How the World Turns

A novel by

Jenny Glazebrook

www.jennyglazebrook.com

Note to my readers

I'm an Australian author which means a few terms may be new to my non-Aussie readers.

Some examples of the differences you may notice in spelling are:

US English   –   Australian English

color   –   colour
honor   –   honour
Savior – Saviour
realize – realise
apologize – apologise
meter   – metre
center   – centre
veranda – verandah
jewelry – jewellery
skeptic – sceptic

I hope you enjoy the authentic Australian characters, dialogue and scenery.

Prologue

Four-year-old Ella shivered, clutching her pink teddy bear close to her chest. The rough boards of the verandah rubbed against her thin dress, splinters catching at loose threads.

She looked up into the night sky. Stars smiled down at her, calling, whispering her name. If only she could float up into the sky and make friends with the shining stars. From here on the back verandah step, it looked as though a koala and a kangaroo sat at a table on the moon, sharing a meal. She'd love to join them. To ask them who made the stars.

She'd asked Daddy who made them. He said God did. Monica laughed and said he was old-fashioned, whatever that meant. But she'd said it in that sweet voice she kept for Daddy, with the smile that never came in Ella's direction.

A cry rang through the house. Verity. Ella squeezed her teddy bear tight. One day, when they were older, she would take Verity to the beach and they would never come back. Maybe they would take Daddy with them. But no, Daddy had to work. All the time.

Monica's voice was screeching now. Like the day Ella had called her Mummy.

"I'll never be your mother," Monica had screamed, rage filling her eyes, turning them dark and scary. "A plain, useless little thing like you? You were made to be hidden. I don't want to see you. I don't want to hear you. Go!"

And Ella had run to this place that had become her refuge. She could look out at the hills, and in her mind she could run, run and be free. The world opened up and she felt alive.

Verity was still crying. Quiet, soft little sobs now. Everything in Ella wanted to go to her, but a quiet voice somewhere up in the stars spoke to her.

Stay. Wait.

It was a gentle voice, but strong and real. She'd heard it a few times now. She didn't know who or what it was, just that there was someone, something bigger than she was out there. Someone who loved her, who saw her, and kept her safe. Maybe there really was a God.

The back door flew open.

"There you are Gabriella."

Ella shrank back. It was never a good thing when Monica used her full name. Her gaze went from Monica's tight expression, down to the suitcase the woman was grasping in one hand and the car keys in the other.

She forced herself to find her voice. "Where ... where are you going?"

Monica leaned down and brought her face close to Ella's, her eyes narrowed, glittering in the dark.

"I'm leaving. I'm not going to sit around wishing for things anymore. I'm going to chase my dreams. One day you'll see me on T.V. A beautiful, famous actress taking the world by storm. And one day I'll come back to get Verity, too. If I hear you haven't looked after her, you will be very, very sorry. Verity is special and she deserves the best. You make sure she gets it, you hear me?"

Ella flinched, shrinking back. She looked up at the stars to find comfort and refuge once more.

Monica laughed, a horrible grating sound. "You think your mother's up there? Watching you? Heaven isn't real, kid. Your mother's gone. Dead."

Ella's throat burned, but she managed to hold back her tears. She'd learned that crying only made Monica angrier.

Monica marched past her, down the steps and toward the car she never let Ella ride in. Ella blinked hard, then she stood. Monica hated her asking questions. Had told her to keep quiet. But right now she needed to. Her voice shook, but she forced the words out.

"Where's Daddy?"

Monica turned back. Her lips tightened into a sneer. "At the pub as usual. And he can stay there forever, for all I care. I've had enough of being stuck in this little town with a husband and screaming children. I was made for so much more."

Ella's chin quivered. She watched Monica's car drive away. Daddy would be so sad that Monica was gone. Monica had made him smile again. At first, anyway.

Did he know Ella and Verity had been left here at home, alone?

You're not alone.

She looked up into the sky. Peace and pain warred within. Monica said she was nothing. Plain and useless.

I love you.

She blinked back tears. She didn't know who or what was there, but the breeze stopped and a warmth wrapped around her heart. Mummy had loved her. Her real Mummy. Daddy told her so. Mummy used to sing her to sleep every night.

Lifting her shoulders, Ella turned and walked bravely back into the house. She would look after Verity. She would love her little half-sister with everything she had and make sure she never felt alone or unloved. Because Ella knew it was an awful feeling. She didn't want anyone she loved to ever experience it.

PART ONE

Chapter One

Why had she agreed to do this? Fifteen-year-old Ella stared out into the audience.

Because Verity had asked her to do it, that's why. And the music teacher had backed her up.

Her tongue felt like chalk. *Swallow,* she told herself. *Just swallow.*

She should never have agreed to sing a solo. Performing was Verity's thing. She should have stayed hidden, behind the scenes where she belonged.

But Verity needed her to do this. Verity was depending on her.

Voices blended in perfect harmony around her as the sounds of the Morley High School choir filled the room. Her heart pounded. Time slowed as the spotlight moved inch by inch toward her and then shone directly in her eyes. She wiped sweaty hands down her shirt. It was time. The final line was hers and she was determined to do it justice.

Swallow. Remember to Swallow.

Taking a deep breath, she allowed her voice to rise up to the ceiling and sing the line that was meant to be Verity's.

"Through sunshine and storm clouds, I'll swallow the road to my dreams."

The moment it left her mouth she knew it was wrong. *Follow.* The word was *Follow.* Fire burned her cheeks. Spotlights blinded her but she could hear the titters of amusement coming from the audience. And then outright laughter. She didn't blame them. Swallow the road?

She was the master of self-sabotage.

Ella slipped backstage and bounded down the stairs to the dressing room. Cold hands tightened around her heart. She grabbed her jacket and pulled it on, hugging it against her chest. The moment played and replayed through her memory like a bad dream. Normally she would have laughed at herself, but this moment had been for Verity.

Thankfully she'd told Dad she didn't want to stay behind for refreshments. He'd be waiting just outside the backstage door, ready to take her home.

The sound of footsteps and talking came from outside and moments later, her friends stumbled into the dressing room.

"There you are, Ella." Willow laughed and shook her head. "You're the star of the show, you realise? No one's ever going to forget that moment."

Ella groaned. "For all the wrong reasons."

"You've got your jacket on inside out." Darcy clicked her tongue. "Here, let me help you."

Before Darcy could touch her, Ella shrugged her arms from the sleeves and let it fall to the floor. Darcy picked it up, shook it out, pulled the sleeves in the right way and placed it back on Ella's shoulders.

"I honestly don't know how you survive in this world, Ella," Willow said, but her smile was affectionate.

"You and me both." Ella let out a hollow laugh. "I should have swallowed a road. Then I couldn't have opened my big mouth and messed that up for everybody."

Darcy's eyes twinkled and Willow covered her mouth, shoulders shaking. "I can just see it," Darcy said.

"Me too." Willow burst into laughter, then wiped at her eyes. "Ella, you're hilarious."

Ella forced a smile. She could see the funny side, she supposed. Everyone knew she was carefree and clumsy, but to mess up in such a big way in front of so many people? When she was doing it for Verity? She sighed. Perfect, beautiful, gifted Verity.

Ella escaped outside to where Dad was waiting. He had that hesitant look, the one that said he didn't quite know what to say or do.

She forced a grin. "Well, I'm glad that's over. At least I know where I fit in the world, now. Or at least, where I don't fit."

Dad tilted his head and studied her. "No more following your dreams?"

"Not onto a stage, that's for sure." She laughed. "I don't know why I let Verity and Mr. Brunskill talk me into singing. Being on stage isn't anything like my dream. I want a nice little cottage in the country, no crowds, just a few animals, a duck pond..." Somewhere she could stay safe and quiet and hidden.

Dad smiled. "Nothing wrong with that plan. I'd do it myself if I didn't need to be close to town for work."

Dad's handyman business kept him busy here in the small country town of Morley. He'd never left the state, let alone Australia, and never planned to. Verity, with her sense of adventure, didn't understand him, but Ella did. She felt the same.

"You do have a lovely voice, Ella," Dad said as they walked to the car. "If you decide you do want to go down the road of singing, all you have to do is work on those nerves."

"And the clumsy thing, and the self-sabotage thing. Nah, it's fine Dad. I wasn't born to be in the spotlight. That's Verity's job."

Dad bit his lip, looking uncertain for a moment. Then he nodded as he unlocked the car. "Okay kiddo, let's head home."

Yes, to their quiet little house on the edge of town. Away from the noise and spotlight. Ella fell into step beside Dad. Their house was especially quiet now, with Verity gone. It had only been a week since Verity left for boarding school in Sydney, but it felt like years. Her sister had an amazing future ahead of her. She was born to stand out. Born to be seen. If only she'd stayed one more week so she could have been the one singing that final line – the way it was meant to be. But once Verity had made up her mind she wanted to go to boarding school, there was no stopping her.

Ella opened the door of Dad's old truck, wincing at the loud creak. She didn't want anyone to notice them, to give her pitying looks or tell her she was wonderful when she knew she wasn't. She didn't need or want their sympathy.

Thankfully no one else had come out of the hall yet. She fell into the front seat, shut the door behind her and looked at Dad. "Let's get out of here."

And pray that no one told Verity what had happened tonight.

Chapter Two

Ella slid into the seat behind Darcy and Willow. Down the back of the classroom where she was most comfortable. It didn't matter that she was always the third wheel. It was good that Willow and Darcy had each other and didn't ever need to feel alone. Ella knew how awful that feeling was and she'd do anything to prevent her good friends from experiencing it.

"Alright class, attention this way." Mr. Dale stood at the front of the room, smiling through his neatly trimmed beard. "We have one more assignment left for the term." His lips tweaked at the groans sounding out around the room. "I know, I know, who would believe you're expected to do work in an economics class?" He handed out a slip of paper. "I want you to think about your future. Think about twenty years from now. Where do you want to be, and how will you get there? I want you to consider how you'll achieve your dream."

Ella winced at the word 'dream'. Thankfully no one looked at her. Except Mr. Dale who caught her eye. Had he just winked at her, or did she imagine it? She sank lower in her seat.

"What steps will you take to follow your dream and turn it into reality?" he asked. "How will you ensure financial sustainability? You have today's lesson to begin and you will present your plans during tomorrow's lesson."

Twenty years? The concert night had confirmed it for Ella. All she wanted was a quiet country cottage just outside of town with some pets. Maybe a few goldfish in a pond in the front yard. Maybe a hobby farm, a husband, and some kids.

How to get there? She was a dreamer, not a planner. She wasn't into business schemes and wealth. Verity was the smart, pretty one. The one made for success. Although, she had to admit her younger sister had become more of a dreamer in the past few months. As soon as Ella told Dad she would like to be a writer, Verity had decided she would become a world-famous author. And she'd proved better at writing with her quick, logical mind and ability with words. So Ella had let go of that dream.

Then when Ella asked Dad if she could go to boarding school because Darcy's parents were thinking of sending her, Dad admitted there wasn't enough money. Ella understood.

But two days later, Verity announced that the small town of Morley didn't have enough opportunities for her and that she wanted to use some of the trust money her mother Monica sent over from the US to go to boarding school.

Dad looked worried. "It's true your mother stipulated this money is to help you follow your dreams," he'd said to Verity. "But … are you sure?"

Verity laughed. "Of course I'm sure. I want adventure. Excitement. Things that Morley can't offer."

And so Dad had arranged to send Verity off to boarding school in Sydney.

"I'm sorry I don't have the money to send you as well," Dad had said to Ella.

She'd smiled. "Don't worry, Dad, it's fine. I don't have any grand dreams like Verity that I need a city education for. And

Darcy doesn't know for sure if she's going to boarding school anyway."

Once Verity left, Ella missed her so much it hurt. She was used to having someone other than herself to care for, to look out for. But now she needed to think about herself. Her own future. Not easy for someone who'd made self-sacrifice into an art form.

***

Ella sat on the verandah that evening, waiting for Dad to come home. She should be finishing her economics assignment, but the house was too quiet and the sunset was too amazing to miss. The sky was streaked with orange and pink. The hills were drying out in the summer sun and in the distance some kangaroos rested beneath a large gum tree. Ella loved the rolling hills. Maybe she'd build her cottage out there. Close enough to see this house, but far enough away to be independent and have her own family.

Her mind conjured up her perfect cottage. Right there on the hillside. And suddenly she itched to draw it. Drawing was something she'd loved until Verity claimed the skill. But Verity wasn't here and Ella was desperate to capture what she saw. She raced inside, grabbed a sheet of paper and a pencil. A picture could paint a thousand words, and Mr. Dale would have to be content with that.

Ella sat back and smiled at her sketch. Her cottage had become more of a mansion, but oh well, the more room, the more children and pets she could have. But then came the hard part of the assignment. How was she going to fund it? Ensure financial sustainability?

She grinned. A rich husband. Chuckling to herself, she grabbed another piece of paper and sketched the face of her imaginary husband, the rich man who would be the free ticket to her dreams. Golden blond hair, blue eyes, a cheeky smile. Her eyes widened as she studied her drawing. It was familiar. Caleb Blake. No! She couldn't let anyone guess the crush she had on him. She screwed the paper into a tight ball and lifted her hand to throw it in the bin. Then stopped. What if Dad found it? She needed to burn it. Completely destroy it.

Taking Dad's lighter from beside his packet of cigarettes in the living room, she set the paper alight, dropped it in the bin and watched it burn out. Smoke wafted up from the ashes, and she waved it away.

She set Dad's lighter back beside his cigarettes, then stilled, her attention caught by a photo in the newspaper Dad had left sitting on the table. The front page featured a family, the father wearing a white coat with a pharmacy label on it. His wife was a beautiful woman. Then there was the son and a daughter. The daughter looked to be in her early twenties, but the son must be around her age.

She could use the features of the pharmacist to create her husband. He was dark-haired and brown-eyed - nothing like Caleb Blake. But no, it felt wrong to use a picture of a married man to inspire her fictitious husband. What about the teenage son? He had a strong jawline and pleasant features. He wasn't smiling, but his eyes were friendly as though he wanted to smile. As though the whole photo taking thing amused him. She could add a beard to his features, a bit of a bald patch and some grey hair around the temples. Perhaps a few lines around the mouth and under the eyes.

Half an hour later she studied her drawing and screwed up her nose. Clearly people were trickier to draw than cottages. The age lines she'd added made the pharmacist's son look cross, not like the good-looking inspiration for her drawing. She studied the photo in the paper again. The guy looked like he laughed freely and enjoyed life. It seemed wrong to make him look so old and frumpy. She'd take the easy way out. Grasping a pair of scissors, she cut around the photo then added a small moustache and goatee. Then she glued him onto a page and sketched a limousine and dollar signs around him, just so people would know he was rich.

"There you go, my husband." She chuckled as she admired her work, then clipped it into her assignment folder along with the drawing of her dream home with seven bedrooms, enough for her ten children and many pets. Assignment done in the usual Ella Glade slap-happy fashion. The less words to express herself, the better. Words belonged to Verity now.

Chapter Three

E lla walked slowly into her economics class the following morning and froze. Horror and disbelief slowly made its way from her heart to her head.

The object of her future plans was sitting beside Willow, the familiar strong jaw and smiling eyes focused on her friend. She knew that jaw, that mouth, those eyes very well. Her pencil had familiarised her with every aspect of his face when she'd tried to draw him. Why hadn't she checked which paper the picture was in? Read the article? She'd assumed it was one of the bigger papers Dad bought, not the local Morley District newspaper.

She darted a look back to the door. Could she make a run for it?

"Hey, Ella." Darcy sat behind Willow and the pharmacist's son, in Ella's usual seat. She pointed to the empty seat beside her.

Sweat slid down Ella's back. She didn't want to be included. Or seen. But everyone was looking at her expectantly.

If only she could think straight. She plopped into the nearest seat, ignoring Darcy. Her mind was a swirling mess of panic and disbelief. It couldn't really be him, could it? Cautiously, she opened her folder and looked at her enhanced photo.

No doubt. It was him. She slammed the folder shut then gasped as pain bit into her finger, caught in the sharp metal ring binder clip. Stifling a cry, she tried to remove her finger. The only problem was the folder required two hands to open the clips and one of hers was trapped in the jaws of the binder. She gritted her teeth, trying to contain her moan, but it slipped out anyway. The whole class turned to look in her direction.

"My finger," she managed. Heat flushed her face as she thought of the drawing being openly displayed for everyone to see.

Mr. Dale strode down the back of the room, released her finger, and studied the blood blister well and truly forming.

"You okay?" A chuckle escaped his lips, followed by an apologetic look. Then he focused on the photo in her folder and his smile morphed into a surprised, puzzled look.

"Is that ... that's Gabriel?"

Gabriel. So that was his name. An interested group had now gathered around and Ella couldn't bring herself to look up.

"I um, I didn't know he would be in our class ..." She glanced at Gabriel. He stared at her with questioning eyes. Eyes that she found fascinating and rather appealing. She shrugged at him and gave a sheepish smile.

He raised an eyebrow and one side of his mouth lifted. Was that amusement? Or something else?

Thankfully Mr. Dale didn't ask her to present her business plan until last, giving her time to recover. She mumbled through the presentation, unable to look at anyone. She skipped over the picture of her imagined—or inspired—future husband and plonked herself back down in her seat.

Mr. Dale looked around the room. "Now I'll be pairing everyone up. Your job will be to plan a business venture together." With a smirk, he looked at Ella. "You can work with Gabriel. Since you think you'd make a good partnership."

Ella felt as though her face were on fire. What was Mr. Dale doing? It wasn't funny. If she had it her way, she'd be avoiding Gabriel for the rest of her life.

"Gabriel and Gabriella," a student called out with a snigger. "Meant for each other."

"Cute," someone else said.

Ella tried to swallow as Gabriel collected his books together and came to sit beside her.

"Actually, I prefer to be called Gabe," he told the class.

"Not a problem." Mr. Dale made a note on his class list. "Gabe it is."

Ella concentrated on opening her notebook and finding a pen, her mind totally void of any sensible words for Gabe. He sat close enough for his arm to brush against hers, so at least he didn't seem to hate her. She felt his eyes on her. Now would be the perfect time to turn invisible.

He bent down to see her face. "So, you got any ideas for a partnership? Apart from marriage, that is?"

Her face burned. "I just needed a picture, that's all," she mumbled. "It was the first thing I found and I didn't know you'd be in our class. I thought ... well," What was she trying to say? "I didn't expect—"

"To meet your dream husband in person so soon?" He said it with a charming, boyish grin and she bit her lip to stop herself smiling.

"Well?" He tapped his pen on the desk, waiting.

"Oh, Gabe, grow a beard." She tried to sound annoyed. Superior. Anything to put space between them and pretend she didn't care that the most embarrassing moment of her life had just occurred.

He pulled a face and looked at the photo of himself with the added beard. "I do look a bit more mature that way, don't I?"

"It suits you." She snapped her folder shut, missing her fingers this time, and tried to hide how vulnerable she felt.

"So tell me about yourself." He looked at her from beneath ridiculously long eye-lashes. No guy had the right to look this good. "I mean, if you're planning to marry me and all ..."

"Don't be ridiculous." She chuckled despite herself.

He kept looking at her, his warm brown eyes twinkling.

She shrugged. "I live in an old house on the edge of town with my dad who's a handyman. My younger sister's at boarding school."

"That's it?"

"Yeah."

"Your mum?"

Ella studied her folder. "My real mum died when I was little."

"Oh no, I'm sorry." She heard the dismay in his voice. Then more quietly, he asked, "Do you remember her?"

"No." But how she wished she did. "I was just a baby. Dad says we were on a flight to visit her parents in Darwin and she had deep vein thrombosis. She went into cardiac arrest." She cleared her throat. "And my stepmother, Verity's mum, is in the US living out her dream of becoming an actress or something."

Gabe's sigh was heavy and heartfelt. "Not a fairy tale life, hey?"

She shrugged as she looked up at him. "Not unless you count Cinderella."

His eyes widened and he chuckled. "At least your nasty stepmother doesn't live with you anymore."

"Yeah, true that."

"But here's hoping for your happily ever after. Which, by the way, I didn't really hear when you were presenting it."

"Not much to hear." She shrugged again, wishing the warmth in her face would dissipate.

He tapped her folder. "Can I see then?"

She looked at him in indecision, then handed it over. "Be careful, it bites."

He laughed, a beautiful free sound that made her heart feel lighter. Then he opened her folder very deliberately keeping his fingers away from the binding clips and studied her pictures. When he finally looked back at her, his dark gaze captured and held hers.

"You're gifted, you know that? I think you could have so much more than a cottage mansion and a bunch of kids."

"What, you think I could have thirty chickens, five cows and a few cats and dogs as well?" She pulled away, laughing as he pretended to swat her with the folder. Then she shook her head, becoming serious again. "The truth is, I don't want more."

He looked back down at her drawing of the cottage, then back at her. "You don't want to be like your stepmother, huh?"

Or take away from her sister's plans and dreams. But how did this stranger understand her so well?

"What about you?" she asked.

"You didn't read the newspaper article about me and my family?"

She crossed her arms over her chest. "I wouldn't have used the photo of you if I had."

He chuckled and tapped his fingers on the photo. "Good point." He closed the folder again. "I have an older sister, Naomi, who's at Uni. My dad's been employed as a pharmacist in the local chemist, which is why we moved here, and my mum's a deacon in charge of pastoral care."

"A what?"

"Like a ... chaplain for the church. She visits sick people in hospital, makes sure everyone's doing okay, prays with them, stuff like that."

"Oh. So she believes in God?"

"My whole family does."

Ella's mind flashed back to lonely times on the back step when she'd felt someone speak to her. Could she ask Gabe about God? Hope rose within. "I think I believe, too."

He smiled at her and something seemed to shift deep inside. She didn't know much about Gabe, but something told her he was going to be in her future.

Chapter Four

Ella startled as the sound of Verity's voice broke through her room.

"Ella! Ellllaaaa!"

She dropped the sketch she'd been working on and grabbed her phone. Verity had thought it was funny when she'd recorded her own voice and changed the ringtone, but she didn't know how that sound set Ella on edge. How it set her heart beating double time, ready to rescue her sister, ready to do whatever it was Verity asked or needed.

Ella caught her breath and answered her phone. "Vee?" She used the affectionate name she'd only been game to use once Monica left. Monica had constantly screamed at four-year-old Ella for struggling to say Verity's name properly.

"Hey, sis. How's everything back at home?"

Ella's shoulders relaxed at Verity's cheerful tone. "Quiet without you. How are you going?"

"Haven't you got something else to tell me first?" Verity sounded put out.

Ella frowned. She and Verity didn't hide secrets from one another. A promise they'd made on Verity's tenth birthday, along with the vow they would never have anything to do with Monica again. Monica had forgotten Verity's birthday that year. For the third year in a row.

But what was Verity referring to? What did she know?

Oh. "You mean the new student at school? He's in a few of my classes. His dad's the new pharmacist in town."

Silence for a beat, then Verity's voice came back, sweet and too casual. "Really? What's his name?"

Ella swallowed hard. She didn't want to share her newfound friendship with Gabe. What was wrong with her? Verity wasn't even here to compete or charm her way into Gabe's life, and leave Ella in the background. That was the thing about Gabe. He made her feel seen. He sat with her in the two classes they shared, and always tried to draw her out of her shell.

"Gabe Vance."

"Hmm. What aren't you telling me, El?"

"There's nothing to tell. He sits next to me in some classes. Why? What did Dad tell you?"

Verity laughed. "Nothing about this friend of yours. He told me about your famous last line on concert night. But it's very telling that you assumed I was talking about this Gabe guy."

Oh no. What had she done? Ella huffed out a sigh. "I made a fool of myself in front of him, that's all. I thought someone must have told you."

"Oh El, what did you do?"

"Found a photo of him in the paper and made him into my dream husband for an assignment, that's all. I didn't know he'd be in my class."

"Trust you to make a terrible first impression." Verity clicked her tongue. "Oh well, there goes any chance of him even glancing at me when I come home."

"At you?" How was this about Verity?

"Yeah, you never know, if I find the right guy I might be willing to give up my dreams of fame and fortune."

Ella knew better than to react. Verity was so competitive. She changed the subject and listened as Verity spoke way above her head about English literature and what techniques she would use to become a famous author. But she knew then that she could never allow herself to admit she was attracted to Gabe. Not now that Verity knew about him. She'd keep her distance, at least emotionally.

***

Ella glanced at Gabe as he took the seat beside her in English. She focused on the front of the room, waiting for the teacher to arrive, but her mind was doing cartwheels. Her phone conversation with Verity last night had left her rattled. She shouldn't have told her about Gabe, about her embarrassing moment with the drawing and the binder.

Gabe's elbow bumped hers. She looked up into dark, smiling eyes. Eyes she convinced herself asked for friendship and nothing more. After all, she was just plain, absent-minded Ella.

"Coming down to the showground tonight?" he asked, adding unnecessary charm to his smile.

"Gabe, I'm trying to do some work."

He put his arm across her textbook so she couldn't see it. "And I'm trying to find out your plans for tonight."

Ella looked away from his olive-skinned arm, from the tendons and strong fingers. And up into his face. She bit her lip to keep from joining in his teasing smile. "You think I'm interested in joining a bunch of drunk teenagers dealing drugs and making fools of themselves?"

He shook his head. "Not the drinking and drugs bit. You don't need it to make a fool—"

She struck him across the knuckles with her ruler and he let out a yelp. The class turned to look and she saw the resigned expressions Willow and Darcy were giving her. Darcy had accused her of dumping them, and Willow accused her of hogging all Gabe's time. Relationships could be such a tightrope to navigate. Ella hated having people unhappy with her, and it was getting harder to please everyone every day.

The teacher came to stand in front of the desk. "What's going on here?"

Ella looked at Gabe who raised his brows back at her. She shrugged. "Just mucking around."

"She hit me."

Oh, so now Gabe decided he had a voice. The teacher's eyebrows lifted in surprise. Ella was never in trouble for bad behaviour. Late assignments and dawdling to class, yes, but she avoided drama and she didn't deal well with attention.

"Don't let her fool you," Gabe said to the teacher, but he was looking at Ella out of the corner of his eye, a mischievous smirk twitching his jaw. "She acts all quiet and shy and sweet, but it's an act."

Ella's jaw dropped. "Really, Gabe?"

"She's actually quite wicked," he called after the teacher who'd lost interest and returned to the front of the room.

Wicked? She leaned close to Gabe. "That's a bit harsh."

He leaned over to whisper back. "I'm trying to help you. You're so scared of getting into trouble that you won't even go out at night and have some fun. Maybe if you get used to getting into trouble you won't be so scared of it."

She snorted. "I'm not going out tonight. I have assignments to finish."

Chapter Five

G abe turned up at her door that night. "Ready to go out?"

"Gabe, I told you I've got assignments to do."

"Please? Just this once. I promise I'll never ask again."

"Yeah, right."

He looked up at Dad, who had come to the door, too. "She needs to get out more, Mr. Glade. And it's my birthday."

"Pfft. It is not." As if she was going to believe that. He'd not mentioned it once at school and she knew him enough to realise he would have made a big deal of it if it was.

His mouth dropped in exaggerated offense. "It is too."

Dad appeared amused by Gabe's pleading and completely taken in by his big brown puppy-dog gaze.

"It'll do you good to go out," Dad said to Ella. "After all, it *is* his birthday."

Dad seemed to trust her completely, sometimes more than Ella thought he should. He'd given Verity and Ella the sex, drugs and alcohol talk a few years ago, and seemed to presume they were sensible enough to take it to heart and do the right thing.

"Where is your party and who is going?" Ella crossed her arms over her chest with a satisfied smile. That would fix him.

"Just a few friends from school." Gabe looked up at Dad. "Willow and Darcy are coming." He tilted his head at Ella. "We'll meet everyone down the main street and decide from there."

Yeah, only one block from the showground. She wasn't fooled one bit. But maybe she did need to get out more. Dad looked so hopeful, like he was worried she wasn't as sociable as Verity, and was relieved that she was invited out with some friends.

She sighed. "Okay, I'll come."

Sure enough, Gabe took her to the showground. Ella wiped clammy hands down her jeans. This was Verity's scene, not hers.

Gabe bumped his shoulder against hers as they made their way to the group of teenagers sitting near the copse of gum trees at the far end of the grounds. "Don't look so worried. You'll have fun. Trust me."

Trust him? When he'd said it was his birthday and lied to her dad? The closer they came to the group, the more Ella's muscles tensed. It was clear that most of them were underage and were drinking. Some laughed unnaturally loud and others swayed on their feet, stumbling against one another.

Someone let out a loud cheer. "Well, look who's here! It's Gabe. And Verity's sister."

Ella tried to slink behind Gabe, but he stepped aside and pulled her by the hand to join their classmates. Ella glanced around. Willow leaned against Darcy, her face red, eyes glazed. Ella had never seen her look like that before.

"Hey, Willow, are you okay?"

Willow didn't answer, but swung an arm out, her elbow glancing off Ella's ribs. Ella backed away, stunned. Had Willow done that on purpose?

"Leave her," Gabe said, taking a can of beer that was offered to him. "She's not a friendly drunk, but she's fine."

He ought to know. Darcy had informed her that Gabe had come to a few of these gatherings.

Gabe opened the can of beer and took a sip while Ella watched in surprise. She hadn't expected Gabe to drink. He was a good student and part of a good, church-going family. And he was underage, like most of the people here.

The more Gabe drank, the more relaxed he became. Ella enjoyed his casual, friendly manner, but she was worried for him. She didn't want him to get into trouble, and she didn't want him to end up drunk and dazed or aggressive, the way Willow was tonight.

"I thought you went to church." She watched as Gabe opened another beer.

He grinned. "'Fraid so."

"Well, doesn't that mean you shouldn't ...?"

He screwed up his nose. "It means my parents don't get drunk and have chosen a religious way of life. I mean, you're not going to be a handyman, are you?"

"No." She took his point. Just because Dad was a handyman didn't mean she wanted to be one too.

"And I'm not religious. I don't believe half that stuff I have to sit and listen to every Sunday."

"But I thought you said you believe in God." She tried to hide her disappointment. She'd been gathering up the courage to ask Gabe some of her burning questions about God.

"Yeah. I do. In my own way."

What did that mean? Ella sat back, trying to process. She liked and trusted Gabe, but tonight it felt like he was trying too hard to fit in. She'd liked that he was different. Like she was. Now she felt alone and left out again, but she wasn't going to drink. She wasn't a rule-breaker.

However, it didn't take long for the pressure to grow. Willow recovered enough from her dazed, drunken state to confront her.

"Got everything you want?" Willow eyed Gabe who was leaning back on the showground's bench seat by Ella's side, his arm resting behind her on the back of the seat.

Ella tried not to feel hurt by her friend's sneering tone. "Yes, thanks."

"So your boyfriend's happy to drink with us, but you're not?"

"Gabe and I aren't —"

"Here. Have a drink then." Willow shoved a bottle of beer at her.

Ella glanced at Gabe, puzzled.

"She clearly doesn't have much logic when she's drunk." Gabe stood and gently pushed Willow back. "Come on Willow, give her some space."

Willow shoved Gabe, then stumbled. Ella flinched as the cold glass of the bottle met her shoulder bone. How was she supposed to deal with Willow when she was like this? It was as if she'd become a different person to the friend Ella had known for so many years.

"Take it," Willow snarled as she waved the bottle aggressively in Ella's face.

"Willow—" She flinched as Willow swung the bottle back. Gabe lurched forward but he wasn't quick enough to block Willow's arm. Thwack. Ella gasped. The pain was overwhelming. She held her cheek. Had something broken? Was it her nose? Voices buzzed around her, but she couldn't make them out for the dizziness fighting to pull her down.

It sounded like Willow was being told off by more than one person. Ella tried to lift her head.

"You idiot," Gabe's voice hissed at Willow.

"You okay?" That was Darcy's voice. She sounded genuinely concerned.

Ella nodded. "I ... I think so." She touched her nose and lip which were now throbbing. It probably wasn't as bad as she'd first thought.

Then Gabe was there, looking into her eyes, regret replacing his previous relaxed demeanour. She felt gentle hands on her face and fought to clear her vision.

"Does it hurt?" His fingers probed gently.

"A bit." But not as much as her heart. Why would Willow do that? Were years of friendship worth less than attraction to a guy? Really?

"I'll get Corey to drive you home." Gabe nodded toward one of the older teens, but Darcy pushed him away.

"No, he's been drinking. I'll walk to the main street with her and call her dad to come and get her."

"Okay." Gabe stepped back.

When Ella's vision cleared and Darcy led her toward the road, she looked back to see Gabe sitting back against the bench again. He gave her a slight wave but she didn't bother to wave back. She was too busy holding her throbbing cheek bone. And Gabe could have offered to come with them. Seeing as he'd insisted on her coming tonight, he *should* have offered to come with her. But he was probably drunk too. Or scared her dad or his parents would find out he was drinking.

Disappointment settled deep within. Gabe Vance was definitely not someone she should fall for. Ever.

Chapter Six

"I guess it's not worth inviting you back down to the showground to celebrate the end of school for the year, right?" Gabe asked as they waited for their roll teacher to hand out end of year reports.

Ella rolled her eyes. He should know better than to ask.

His lips tilted. "I have to admit your black eye was impressive."

"Yeah, well, I don't think your parents would want you going down there either." He'd told her how Willow had hit someone else with a beer bottle last week. It was surprising the local police hadn't shut down the area already. Surely they knew what was going on?

"Maybe not, but my life's my own." He shrugged. "But if Mum and Dad happen to ask you about me coming over to do homework at your place once a week, I need you to cover for me."

Ella's mouth dropped open. "You'd use me as your cover?"

"My parents like you."

"They've only seen me once." When she'd come over to their place in her trackie pants and football jersey. Mr. Vance was a serious, formal kind of man while Gabe's mother was poised and beautiful. They'd been warm and welcoming but she'd wondered what they thought of her. She was no Verity.

"I don't want to lie to them." Ella bit the side of her lip. "And I don't want to feel guilty every time I see them because I'm hiding something from them."

"Oh, you're such a worrier." Gabe gave her an affectionate side hug. "If my parents don't know then they're clearly not keeping a close enough eye on me. That's on them, not on you. You're not my mother." He grimaced. "Although you act like you are, sometimes."

It was true. It helped her keep her distance. Helped hide her growing feelings for her best friend.

"Gabriella Glade?" the teacher handing out the reports called.

Ella went forward. The report felt heavy in her hand. She hated this time of year. And this year she couldn't focus on Verity and rejoice at her good grades instead. She opened the envelope on her way back to Gabe, glanced at the first page and groaned.

"What's up?" Gabe asked.

"My marks are pitiful."

"I'm sure they're not." Gabe looked over her shoulder. Then he widened his eyes and covered his mouth in pretend shock. "Wait, they really are, aren't they?"

She pushed him in the chest. A chest growing more solid by the day as he filled out his tall, lanky frame. It made it harder to remember to treat him like a child.

"Gabriel Vance," the teacher called.

Gabe shot her a grin as he sauntered down the front to collect his report. She tried not to make it obvious she was watching his every move, but it was hard not to.

He ripped his report from the envelope and came back, frowning down at it. "Pitiful," he groaned.

She doubted that. "Show me."

He shoved it back in the envelope. "No, sorry. It's too awful."

"Yeah, right." She knew he'd topped almost every class despite his lax attitude and he'd excelled in athletics as well. She eyed the envelope he held. Could she snatch it from him? His hand tightened over the paper and she glanced up. His look was knowing and amused at once. There was no chance she was going to see his report.

"You realise your marks don't matter?" He tapped her on the head with his report. "It's your heart that counts, who you are inside."

"Right. Says who?"

"My parents." He shrugged. "God. The Bible."

Really? Then she groaned. He was just trying to make her feel better. "That's like saying someone's nice, isn't it? There's always a but after it. You're nice, but ..."

He frowned. "No, that's not what I'm saying."

It was. He was just too nice to admit it. "I just wish there was one subject I was good at, that's all. Just one."

"You should've taken art."

She should have. But she hadn't known how much she loved it before she'd chosen her senior subjects.

"I could help you with your running if you want. Become your running coach."

Hope filled her, but she pushed it away. "As if. It would take too much time out of your social life."

His eyes widened. "Oh Ella, don't you know I only seek out a social life because you're too busy for me? Always doing homework, helping your dad, drawing ... What else am I supposed to do when my best friend is distracted?"

Was he serious? She couldn't tell, but if training her would keep him from going to the showground and getting drunk it would be worth it.

She held out her hand. "You're on. I am officially hiring you as my coach."

He shook her hand then pulled her in for a hug, holding his report behind her back. "We've got this, Gabriella. You and me, final year senior athletics champions."

His hug left her overwhelmed, confused. She pulled back. "Deal."

***

Gabe trained Ella as promised. He was merciless, making her run until she could run no more.

"It's all for your good," he said as she lay on the ground moaning. Her legs were killing her.

"Come on, get up and keep going," he said as he pushed her with the toe of his shoe. "Got to build up those muscles, make a man out of you." He flexed his muscles, grinning down at her.

"Oh Gabe, grow a beard."

He laughed at the affectionate insult she used on him every chance she got. "If you want to be the best, you've got to out-train the best."

He was right. They both made it to regional athletics for the one and two hundred-metre sprints. Ella didn't tell Verity until the day before the event.

At first her confession was met with stunned silence. "You didn't tell me," Verity finally said, her tone accusing.

"What, and give you the chance to outdo me in athletics, too?" Ella laughed. "No, Vee, it's my turn to achieve. You keep your academic medallions and I'll get my athletic ones."

Verity laughed too, but it sounded strained. Ella worried that she may have hurt her and told Gabe so.

"Don't you worry about her," he said. "Tomorrow is your day. I mean, yours and mine. Let's make it a day we never forget."

Chapter Seven

Ella sat beside Gabe as they travelled to the nearest town for the athletics carnival. Why was she so nervous? It wasn't like they'd made it to State or National level.

Gabe looked down at her hands. "You okay?"

Oops. She hadn't realised she was tearing her fingernails apart. "I guess so."

He placed his hand over hers. "Breathe deep. It helps."

She stilled. He didn't move his hand away and she looked up at him. He raised his brows. "I'm waiting."

She rolled her eyes and drew in a deep breath.

"See? Better already." He smiled and a tingly warmth fluttered in her chest. Sitting here with Gabe so close beside her, his shoulder resting against hers, looking at her this way ...

"So are you two an item or what?" Caleb Blake's voice startled her from behind. He poked his head between the seats of the bus.

Heat rose up into Ella's face. Gently, she pulled her hand out from beneath Gabe's.

"What kind of item?" Gabe asked. "Food item, prohibited item, item of interest ..."

"Funny, aren't you?"

"Caleb, put your seat belt back on."

Ella's shoulders sagged with relief at the teacher's order. She might have once had a crush on Caleb, but that had faded when ... well, around the time Gabe had moved to town.

All too soon they arrived at the venue.

"Oh no," Gabe moaned as they descended the steps of the bus. "There's my mum."

Ella chuckled at his 'misfortune'. How could he be ashamed of his mother? How could he not want her there? She was beautiful, poised, and compassionate. Gabe didn't know how lucky he was.

Ella gave his shoulder a playful shove. "Blow her a kiss."

He screwed up his nose, giving her what was supposed to be a disgusted look, but the twitch of his lips gave him away. He didn't really mind his mother being there. He wandered over to meet her and Ella watched with envy. It was times like this she missed her own mother. Not that she could remember her. The only mother figure she'd had was Verity's mother. A woman who slapped Ella every chance she had and screamed at her whenever her father wasn't around. She made sure Ella knew she would never match up to Verity.

If a woman like Margo Vance was her mother, she would treasure her every day of her life.

Her race was called over the loudspeaker before she'd had time to get her bearings. Gabe looked up from where he stood talking with his mother and gave her a quick wave. Drawing in a deep breath, Ella headed for the start. Standing in the blocks, she focused on the finish line. This was her chance, her one chance to prove she could be good at something. She would never do it academically, so it had to be this way.

Dad couldn't be here because he had to work, but he'd promised he would be thinking of her all day. She needed to make

Dad proud of her, to convince herself that her stepmother's words weren't true. She wasn't useless.

She tensed, waiting for the starter pistol. Her legs shook and adrenaline surged through her veins.

The pistol cracked and Ella only just heard it against the hammering of her heart. She leaped forward, feeling the power in her muscles as she pushed her legs. She felt alive and strong and knew she was doing well. Elation surged, knowing she was in the lead. Finally, she'd prove them—

Oh! Her world tilted and she found herself on the ground. Pain tore at her ankle.

Through eyes blurred with agony and tears she saw the girl coming first over the finish line. The complete and utter disappointment added to the pain in her ankle.

An official squatted beside her. "Are you okay?"

Ella nodded, biting her lip. She was helped up and supported as she limped off the track and to the first aid tent. She couldn't bear to look up, knowing everyone would be looking at her.

She fell into the chair provided and a familiar face came into focus.

Gabe's mother. Eyes like Gabe's looked down at her, filled with compassion and understanding. It was Ella's undoing. Tears of pain, embarrassment and disappointment leaked from her eyes.

"Oh Ella," Mrs. Vance's comforting arms came around her shoulders. "You ran so well. You should be proud of yourself."

She placed a soft kiss on Ella's hair then handed her a tissue to wipe her tears. Warmth filled Ella, a healing balm to her heart. She took a deep breath, soaking in the genuine compassion and encouragement.

How could Gabe be embarrassed by his mother? If Ella had a mother like this, she'd cling to her with everything she had.

Mrs. Vance then knelt on the ground in front of her, not seeming to care that she was wearing a beautiful pant suit that would get dirty.

"Do you mind if I take a look at your ankle?"

Ella shook her head as Mrs. Vance gently removed her shoe and sock, then inspected her ankle while explaining to the school's athletic coach that she was trained in first aid and had once been a nurse. That was news to Ella.

Margo Vance smiled at Ella. "That's how I met my husband. Our first jobs were in the same hospital." She gently prodded the area around Ella's fast-swelling ankle. "It's sprained," she said, requesting a bandage from the first aid tent, then strapping it tight.

The coach looked down at her. "No running the two hundred metres for you today, I'm afraid," he said apologetically.

Ella nodded, then glanced at Mrs. Vance. "Thank you for your help. But please, go and watch Gabe. His race is about to start."

"He'll be okay." Her smile was wry. "He's embarrassed I'm even here."

"Or he pretends to be." Ella winced as she shifted her ankle. "Please go and watch him. If I had my mother …" She shrugged. "Whether he knows it or not, he needs you to be there."

Mrs. Vance's eyes softened. "You're a treasure, Ella Glade."

With that, she left to find Gabe.

Ella watched her go. Mrs. Vance was the treasure. Her son wasn't too bad, either.

***

"You okay?" Gabe pulled up an empty chair in the first aid tent and sat facing her. His first race was done and Ella knew his mother must have filled him in on her accident. She gave him a lopsided smile. "I'm fine. You?"

He shrugged. "Well, I didn't win, but I managed to get through without injury."

She pulled a face. "Rub it in, why don't ya? You don't have your mother's compassion, that's for sure."

"Sorry. I didn't mean —"

"Hey, I was just stirring." She hadn't meant to make him feel bad.

He studied her a moment before his lips lifted and he dropped to his knees beside her. He took her hand in his and reached up with his other to stroke her hair. "Oh, you poor thing. I'm so sorry this has happened to you. Where does it hurt? Can I carry you anywhere?"

He put an arm beneath her knees to lift her, but she slapped him away, laughing to hide the confusion swirling within. What was it that made her whole body respond to his touch? It was too much, her senses overwhelmed.

She shoved him. "Go and stretch before your next race, you clown."

"No, really, I am sorry," he said, his tone serious again as he sat back in the chair. "But you don't have to prove yourself, you know that, don't you? In the big scheme of things, this isn't going to change your life. Yes, you put a lot of training in, but really, who you are matters a whole lot more than winning a race."

"Really? Says the one who trained me, who is a natural at everything he does."

"Not running." He looked away and she caught something in his expression.

"What do you mean?"

He hesitated then looked down at his running shoes. "I only do well in athletics because I trained my heart out back in primary school. I learned all the techniques, even got my parents to pay for coaching for me. I did it out of desperation."

Ella frowned. "I don't understand."

"Smart boys weren't popular in my old school, Ella." He looked up at her again. "There was this whole tough boy culture where you had to be strong and fast and good at sport if you wanted to fit in. And not be bullied."

"You were bullied?" Dismay filled her at the thought of anyone hurting him.

"Yeah, just the normal rough and tumble stuff, and a bit of ridicule, but it still hurt. I guess I just don't want to see you change or be consumed by something because you don't feel like you're good enough." His eyes locked on hers and his voice softened. "Because you are."

What was she supposed to say to that? She fought the warmth filling her face. "When's your next race?"

He gave her a long look, but didn't call her out on the abrupt change of subject. Then he stood. "I'll check back in on you later."

"Thanks. And all the best, Gabe. I hope you win. I really mean that."

He gave her a quick nod and wave as he jogged back toward the oval.

If only she'd been able to say what she was really thinking. That he didn't need to prove himself either. He was smart and charming and fun and his good looks completed the picture. He was more than good enough the way he was.

Chapter Eight

Ella sat on the back verandah with Gabe in the coolness of twilight, trying to put Verity's latest phone call from her mind and failing dismally.

"Earth to Ella. Where are you?" Gabe nudged her with his elbow.

She tried to smile but it came out as a sigh. "Verity has joined her school athletics team."

"And that's a problem because ...?" He waited, eyebrows raised.

"Because she's never been interested in athletics before. Or sport. Or anything like it. She just can't help outdoing me. She was born to win."

Gabe leaned back on his hands. "Sounds to me like she's jealous of you. They say imitation is the highest form of flattery."

Or something. Ella blew out a breath. Verity would be home in a few weeks for the holidays and everything would change. She needed to enjoy time with Gabe now, while she could. And then she would need to focus on Verity. The way she always had.

A flash of light zipped across the sky. Ella gasped and straightened. "Did you see that?" Her heart was pounding.

"See what?" Gabe followed her gaze up into the sky.

"A shooting star." A sign of hope. A reminder that life was bigger than her and all her problems.

"Nope."

Maybe it was her imagination. She stared up into the night sky, appreciating that Gabe was with her, but wishing he understood what even she didn't understand. That longing deep inside to know that someone really was out there, looking out for her, seeing her. Caring.

"Where do you think heaven is?" She turned to look at Gabe, the outline of his face now shadowed by the night sky.

He shrugged. "Up there somewhere, I suppose."

"Do you think our lost loved ones are up there?"

Even in the darkness she saw the way he winced. He didn't believe. He didn't share that deepest longing she felt somewhere inside to know there was eternity. That life wasn't empty, here today and gone tomorrow. She couldn't handle hearing him voice it, couldn't wait for his answer. She rushed on to change the subject, not giving herself time to think before she spoke.

"Sometimes I sit out here and look up at the sky to get inspiration for my sketches."

She immediately had his attention. What had she done? She'd *never* meant to tell anyone about her sketches, about how her slap-happy attempt at the economics assignment had awakened in her a love of art. She loved the way people's faces came to life in her mind and transferred to her fingertips where she re-created everything she saw.

"What do you sketch?"

Him. Her mum, her dad, Verity. All the people she knew and loved. "Just stuff."

"Can I see?"

Did she trust him? That was the question. Did she have any safe work she could show him? Anything good enough for him to see, but not so close to her heart she'd feel rejected if he didn't like it?

"I have a sketch of Verity I can show you." She stood. "You stay here." Far away from her sketch pad and all the portraits of him.

She ran inside and pulled out her sketch pad, sifting through all the portraits. There. One of Verity smiling, eyes sparkling with joy, a sign of Ella's success. Even her step-mother would have to admit Ella had done a good job of making Verity happy. She carefully tore it from the book and headed back out to the verandah and Gabe.

Gabe put down his phone, giving her his full attention. She switched on the back porch light and came to sit beside him. Why was she so nervous? With a deep breath she handed over Verity's portrait.

His eyes widened and he let out a long breath. "Wow."

'Wow' she was gifted, or 'wow' Verity was pretty? She tensed, waiting for him to say something else. She'd wanted this reaction, hadn't she? But now she wasn't sure what to make of it.

"Have you done any of me?" he asked, finally drawing his eyes from the picture and looking at her.

She didn't want to lie. But she couldn't let him know the truth either. Her mind scrambled for what to say. "Why ... why would I do that?" Not a lie, but she hadn't meant her tone to sound scornful.

"Because we're friends." His brow furrowed and she wished she could smooth away the lines.

"I'll do one of you," she promised. After all, it was okay to do if he'd kind-of asked. No need for him to know she already had a sketch pad full of his likeness inside.

"Can you do one while I watch?"

Huh. She blinked against the light, heart pounding. No. No, she couldn't draw him while he was looking at her like that. It was hard enough to meet his eyes while strange feelings raged inside her, a longing to be close, yet a fear as well.

He picked up on her hesitation. "What about the view then? Can you draw one of the stars?"

"I have already." She took the chance to escape. "I'll go and get it."

He was staring up into the sky when she returned. He took the sketch from her hands, studied it, then looked directly at her. "You've got a gift," he said, his voice deep, a husky note to it. "Such a gift." He cleared his throat and gazed out into the night again. "I wish I knew what my gift is."

He didn't know? "Gabe, you're so good at everything. You can do whatever you want."

"Can I?" He turned and looked at her. The way his eyes searched hers left her mouth dry.

"What do you want?" Her voice came out in a whisper.

"I want to take you to the Halley's Comet viewing party."

"The what?"

His fingers tapped across his phone screen, then he held it out to show her. "It's an event on Facebook. Look, it's a Halley's Comet Viewing Party. In 2061."

"2061?"

His smile held warmth. "Halley's Comet only comes around every eighty years or something and I want you and I to still be friends. I want us to go together."

"I wouldn't have thought you could create a Facebook event so far in advance." But there it was. Ella skimmed the details. "Namadgi National Park in Canberra in July? It'll be freezing."

"So we'll bring a blanket. Snuggle up together to keep warm."
Her cheeks warmed at the image. "Sounds like a plan."

Chapter Nine

Ella dawdled to class on the last day of school. There were still the final exams and the formal to go, but she had received an early offer into a fashion design course. She should be excited, but her heart was heavy. Verity had laughed when she'd told her about the course offer.

"Ella, you have the worst sense of fashion of anyone I've ever met."

She was right, but it was the only course offering early entry that allowed her to draw, to sketch people and faces. It had become her favourite thing to do. No one knew how many portraits of Gabe she now had hidden in her bottom desk drawer. Gabe smiling. Gabe trying not to smile. Gabe laughing with abandon. Gabe looking concerned. Gabe frowning. With each tender stroke of her pencil she'd felt closer to him, but it was dangerous.

She'd be heading to Sydney for her course and Gabe was planning to go to Melbourne to complete a business degree. She would miss him when he was gone, but they'd keep in touch. They had to.

She wandered into the classroom and hesitated. Willow was sitting beside Gabe, where Ella usually sat.

Gabe shot her an apologetic smile. With a shrug, she sat down the front of the room and slowly opened her books. If she was honest, she'd been hoping Gabe would ask her to be his partner at their end of year formal. Maybe Willow had taken advantage of Ella's lateness to ask Gabe to go with her, instead.

Something hit her desk. With a start she jerked back, then picked up the permanent marker. Gabe.

The teacher looked in her direction and she closed her hand over the marker.

"Excuse me, Miss. Ella has a permanent marker." Gabe's laughing voice came from the back of the room. "Can she be expelled for having contraband on her last day?"

Ella let out a scoffing noise. "I may have a permanent marker, but where did it come from, Gabriel Luke Vance?"

Gabe sat up straighter. "Ooh, resorting to full names now. Someone feels threatened. And what makes a person feel threatened and become defensive? Guilt, that's what."

The teacher looked between them. Then her lips tilted in a bemused smile. "Your poor Uni lecturers. I feel for them already."

"What do you mean, Miss?" Gabe pretended to look hurt. "I can't believe you would imply that you haven't loved having me in your class. And on the last day, too."

"Hmm." The teacher turned back to the front of the room.

Gabe waved his hand in the air. "Hey, doesn't Ella get in trouble for having the marker?"

Ella let out a scornful laugh. "Oh, grow a beard, Gabe Vance."

He raised his eyebrows and grinned. She couldn't help smiling back, annoyed with herself for finding that boyish grin so irresistible. She needed to distract herself by planning revenge. He deserved it.

The recess bell rang. Students scrambled to leave the classroom, but Ella took her time packing her bag. Once the room had emptied, she went to the whiteboard out the front. Taking the whiteboard marker from the teacher's desk, she began a quick sketch. Gabe Vance with a moustache, beard and devil's horns for good measure. In front of his image she placed jail bars and the words, "Good luck for your future."

She stepped back, her mouth stretching into a grin. He deserved it.

Footsteps pounded down the hallway and with reflexes like lightning, she dropped the marker.

But not quickly enough.

Gabe stood just inside the door, looking at her. "What are you doing in here?"

She raised wide, innocent eyes, and stepped away from the board. "I should be asking *you* that question."

"I came to see what was taking you so long."

"You know I take forever to pack up." She made sure she stood in front of his picture on the whiteboard, blocking his view as best she could.

He stepped closer. "What are you up to?" His voice was suspicious and knowing all at once.

He took another step forward and that's when he saw the picture over her shoulder. She watched his eyes widen and his mouth form an O. Then he looked down at her.

She challenged him with her eyes, lifting her chin slightly. "I thought the world needed to know what to expect from you in the future."

"You thought that, did you?" He took another step closer, so close he was almost touching her.

She backed away. "I did. But I'll clear it off now."

She grabbed the whiteboard eraser and began wiping the board with great flourishing strokes. Until his hand stopped hers.

"Wait. It's actually a very good picture. It would be a pity for people not to see it." He picked up the whiteboard marker. "And to not know you drew it."

He wrote her name beneath the picture. Then added the words, "Gabriella Glade's dream husband."

"Hey!" She couldn't help laughing as she tried to pry the marker from his fingers. He held it above his head. She jumped, but it was futile. He was too tall.

She gave him her fiercest mock glare and he merely smiled, his eyes twinkling as they held hers.

"I'm going to miss you, Ella Glade," he said, and his face softened.

She swallowed hard. Was he about to ask her to come to the formal with him? Because her answer would be yes.

He opened his mouth, closed it again. Then suddenly, as though impulse overtook him, he stepped forward and brushed his lips against hers.

She froze. What was he doing?

His arms came around her, drawing her close and her heart pounded, imprisoned against his chest. She stared at his lips as they descended again, claiming hers with more determination this time. She gasped in shock.

She needed to escape. To think. She couldn't deal with this rush of new sensations coursing through her. Panic set in, nothing was making sense, and she pushed back against his chest, staring up at him. "What are you doing?" Her voice came out in a whisper.

He chuckled. "I think it's pretty obvious."

His head lowered again, but she leaned away. She needed space, time to process, to disguise the vulnerable feelings assailing her. It was too overwhelming.

"Gabe ..." She couldn't look at him as her gaze darted around the room, searching for something solid to land on, something real to hold onto, because this couldn't be real. "I don't understand. Why would you ... I thought ... "

His arms dropped to his side, releasing her. She looked up and caught a glimpse of the hurt that flashed through his eyes. Then his expression shuttered as he shrugged and pulled a face. "I just wanted to see if your lips are as cold as that look you're giving me."

What? How could he say that? A first kiss wasn't supposed to be like this, was it? What was wrong with her? Why was she so afraid of showing him how she felt?

She drew in a shaky breath, trying not to cry. "Well, now you know."

"I guess I do."

***

Ella charged from the classroom and hid in a cubicle in the girls' toilets. With trembling fingers, she touched her lips, still tingling from Gabe's kiss. Questions swarmed her mind. What had she done? Why couldn't she be normal and respond to affection like every other girl she knew? Was Gabe in love with her? She'd never thought it possible. Not really. But he'd kissed her. What did that mean? It *had* to mean he had feelings for her beyond friendship, didn't it?

She hadn't dared hope. Hadn't dared dream. But what did this mean for their future? She needed to talk to him. To apologise. Explain that he'd shocked her, that was all. That maybe he could give her a second chance.

But when she finally left her hiding place, he wasn't in her next two classes. Where was he? She'd have to try to catch him at the end of school.

The end of school. Why had he waited until their final day? Why hadn't he said anything earlier? Soon they'd be separated by distance and unable to explore what could be between them. Although they still had another few months before they left for Uni which should give them time to talk. To work out a deeper relationship and what that meant. To explore romance.

Romance. Her skin prickled. She hadn't had a good example, growing up without her mother and then having a stepmother who didn't love her or her dad. But Gabe's parents clearly loved each other. Perhaps Gabe could guide them. She should be able to trust him. He knew what a real, loving relationship looked like. But could she believe it was even possible?

Her heartbeat doubled and she blinked hard against the doubts. Gabe Vance loved her. Intelligent, warm-hearted, charming Gabe with the irresistible smile loved *her*. It was a dream come true.

"Gabe!" She raced after him as he headed out the school gate that afternoon.

He stopped to look behind him, his expression hesitant and unsure. She'd done that to him. Made him think she was angry with him, that she didn't welcome his kiss.

"Can you come to my place this afternoon? I need to talk to you about ..." She looked at the students milling around and lowered her voice. "About what happened."

He glanced toward his bus pulling into the bus zone. "It's okay, Ella. You don't need to explain. I understand."

No. No, he didn't. "Please. Just come."

He pressed his lips together, then shrugged. "I'll see."

Chapter Ten

Ella charged in the front door, relieved to finally be home. Relieved to have time to sort out her swirling thoughts. Surely Gabe would come. He had to. He wouldn't assume she didn't have feelings for him, not from her reaction to one kiss, would he? Well, not from one kiss. If she was honest, whenever he looked at her tenderly or showed affection, she put walls up or completely froze. Not because she didn't enjoy it or even want it, but because it scared her. Dad was great, and she knew he loved her, but he wasn't affectionate. She simply didn't know how to respond to affection from anyone apart from her sister. And she didn't want to entertain hopeless dreams.

"Ella!"

She started at the sound of her sister's voice. She reached for her phone before she realised it wasn't her phone.

Verity was running toward her, a huge smile lighting her beautiful face. "I told Dad not to tell you I was coming. I wanted to surprise you."

"Vee!" Ella hugged her tight. She had to be dreaming. "Why are you home?"

Verity pouted prettily. "Don't you want me here?"

"Of course I do. I've missed you!"

Verity beamed. "I wanted to be here for your formal, to celebrate with you, so Dad said I could come home for a few days."

Ella's heart sank. "But we aren't allowed to bring siblings. We're only supposed to bring partners or parents."

"So let me be your partner."

"I don't think sisters count as a partner." And what made her assume she didn't already have a partner? Because if things went as she hoped they would with Gabe ...

Verity's face fell. Then she brightened. "Oh well, maybe all your friends will go out afterwards. I'll go with you to make you feel more comfortable."

Again, who said she wanted to go out, or that she wouldn't feel comfortable on her own? It annoyed her that Verity knew her so well. And yet, "Okay," she heard herself say.

Verity's blue eyes sparkled and Ella was relieved she'd managed to placate her. Verity had grown taller and looked more sophisticated and beautiful than ever. Her hair was tied back in a messy pony-tail that she managed to make look fashionable. Her well-fitting jeans and cute top showed off her model-like figure.

"Hey, you're as tall as me," Ella said, pretending to be upset by the fact.

Verity laughed her sweet, musical laugh. "Had to happen someday, El."

Ella's heart warmed and any irritation she'd felt faded away. No one else in the world called her El with that same affection and familiarity. How she'd missed her sister. With another cry of delight she hugged her again.

Then they sat on the lounge and Verity began talking. About the drama course she'd taken at school, about her writing, her new dream of being a model, of the world that lay at her feet.

Ella listened, trying to keep up with Verity's changing dreams.

Footsteps sounded along the verandah and Verity paused in her monologue.

"Who's that?"

"Hello?" came Gabe's familiar voice.

Ella's heart pounded. Now what? She really needed to talk with Gabe, but she also needed to pretend nothing was amiss in front of Verity. She couldn't have Verity knowing what had happened between her and Gabe at school today.

She called to him from where she sat. "Gabe? My sister's home."

His deep chuckle floated through the door. "So, do I get to come in and meet her or do I have to stay out here?"

Ella rolled her eyes, fighting to appear casual. "What other time have you asked to come in? Don't pretend to be all polite, now."

He chuckled again as he wandered in. "Come on, I'm trying to make a good impression—"

He stepped in the door and stopped short, his gaze fixed on Verity. Verity stood, her smile full and stunning, her beautiful eyes wide and welcoming.

Ella saw the look that passed between them. A look that said something significant, something life-changing was occurring. A look that said the world had just shifted for both of them.

"So you're Verity," Gabe managed to say, and there was something in his voice that Ella had never heard before.

"Verity Monica Glade."

His eyes crinkled in the corners. "You want me to call you by your full name?"

Verity blushed deep red. Ella blinked. Was that real? Verity was always composed. Completely together.

"No, I just thought you should know my full name."

He smiled. "Okay, so what's your nickname? Very? Itty? Very Breathtaking, or Very Stunning?"

Heat rose in Ella's chest and she cut in. "Gabe, don't pick on her already. You've only just met her."

She didn't have to pretend to be annoyed. She truly was. Only hours earlier he'd kissed her and now he was flirting with her sister? Was he trying to make a point? Was he showing her that not everyone treated him as condescendingly as she did? She hadn't meant to, and if he'd just give her a chance to explain ...

Gabe ignored her and Ella watched, her heart dipping, as his eyes fixed on the blushing Verity. Could Verity really be feeling self-conscious, or was she being coy? Ella had never seen her react this way to anyone.

She looked at Gabe through Verity's eyes. He was all charm and masculinity as he began asking questions, drawing Verity out of herself and discovering her deepest thoughts and dreams. He seemed enraptured when Verity gushed about her life achievements, the things she loved, the things she hated.

"So you're home for the holidays?" Gabe asked Verity.

"No, just for a few days. I wanted to be here for Ella's formal, but she tells me it's only for students, their parents and partners."

"That's true, but you could come as *my* partner."

Ella stared at Gabe, managing to keep her jaw from dropping. Seriously? She waited for him to look at her, but his eyes were fixed on Verity.

"You mean it?" Verity asked breathlessly.

"Of course." He laughed as Verity threw her arms around his neck then danced and squealed with delight. It was clear he was captivated by everything about her.

Something inside Ella died. Gabe didn't even notice when she slipped out the front door.

Verity had done it again. Competed and won. And for the first time it broke her heart.

Chapter Eleven

Verity came home again for the summer holidays and this time they were long and lonely. Gabe and Verity only had eyes for each other. Something had happened between them at the end-of-year formal and Ella couldn't help resenting that Verity had been there. Once again, Verity had outshone her. She'd been stunning and every person in the room, especially Gabe, had not been able to keep their eyes off her. What was this hold Verity had over Gabe? Over everyone she met? Because if Ella was honest, Verity had that same hold over her. Everyone lived to please Verity. To make her happy.

To some extent Ella understood why she lived that way. Dad had struggled when Monica left, and Verity had relied on her from an early age as a mother figure. That meant making sure Verity was loved, protected and happy. Wasn't that what mothers were supposed to do? Verity shouldn't have to miss out on a mother just because Ella had.

But why was Gabe living to please Verity? He didn't owe her anything. It just proved what Ella had always suspected. Verity was special. She was beautiful, gifted, and made for great things. She supposed she should feel honoured that she'd played a part in making Verity what she was.

But Gabe? He'd played no part in that.

"Come on, Gabe," Ella challenged him the morning after Verity had given her all the details of her first kiss with Gabe, long and tender and clearly reciprocated. "She's still at boarding school. She's young and she never commits to anyone or anything for long. She has so many big hopes and dreams for her future. You don't really think she'll commit to a long-distance relationship, do you?"

"You think I'm not good enough for her, either, do you?"

The hurt in his tone left Ella taken aback. "I've never thought you're not good enough."

"Really?" His eyes darkened. "You've treated me like some naughty little schoolboy since the day we met, and then when I tried to show you how I felt, you made it very clear you don't feel the same."

Ella swallowed hard. "I didn't mean ..."

Her words dried. How could she explain it to him? That he'd taken her by surprise? That she'd thought he might ask her to come to the formal with him and had been stunned when he kissed her instead. She didn't know how to respond to affection and had never dared hope he would feel that way about her.

"What didn't you mean?"

She opened her mouth to try to explain, but Verity came in, went straight to Gabe, pulled his head down and kissed him.

Staking her claim.

Verity finally acknowledged that Ella was in the room. "What are you two talking about?" She tipped her head and smiled, everything about her stunning and sweet rolled into one.

Except Ella suspected that wasn't sweetness. Verity knew what she wanted and no one was going to get in her way.

"Nothing. It doesn't matter." Gabe put his arms around Verity's waist and smiled into her eyes.

Verity tossed a look at Ella over his shoulder that was part triumph, part challenge. Was this a game to her? Well, Ella wasn't playing. Gabe Vance needed to fight his own battles, make his own choices. No matter how much Ella regretted the choice he made and her part in leading him there.

***

"I don't think I want to go back to boarding school for year eleven and twelve," Verity told Dad as the new year approached. "I've discovered it's not what I really want after all."

Dad rubbed his chin. "I wondered if that might prove the case. What would you like to do?"

"I want to leave school and do a college course. I found a great one in Melbourne close to Gabe's Uni, so we can spend more time together. It's a Diploma of Fashion Design and Merchandising."

Fashion Design? Ella gritted her teeth. She would not compete with Verity. She would change her Uni course. Maybe apply for a Bachelor of Fine Arts. She hadn't studied art at school, but maybe they'd accept the sketches she'd been working on these past few years as her portfolio. It was time she took a risk and chased her dreams.

"Where would a course like that take you?" Dad asked Verity.

Ella's question exactly.

"I don't know. Maybe I could work from home, come up with designs in my own creative space. A quiet little house in the country somewhere with Gabe would be a perfect place to inspire amazing designs." She giggled. "When we get married, of course."

Ella wanted to be sick. She approached Dad that evening when Verity was once more out with Gabe. "Dad, are you really going to let Verity throw away her future for a high school crush?"

Dad looked up, pushing the stub of his cigarette into the ash tray. "You don't think she loves him?"

"How can she? She's only just met him."

Dad's eyebrows lifted. "I thought you of all people would be the one to understand."

"Understand? This is what I understand. Verity is smart, she has so much potential, but she's too young to know what she really wants. She was born to stand out, to be something special and it would be sad for her to waste her potential because she fancies herself in love."

"Are you hearing yourself Ella?"

Yes, yes she was. But was he hearing *her*? "Dad, we gave her everything so she can reach the top, so she can achieve her dreams." Or she had, anyway. "She doesn't want a quiet life in the country with a husband and kids. She wants so much more. That's why she left to go to boarding school, remember?"

Dad slumped in his seat. "Ella, the older I get, the more I realise that family should come first. Love is the essence of life. When you are on your death bed, I don't think you'll be looking back saying, 'I wish I made more money. I wish I did better with my career.' No, Ella, you'll be wanting your loved ones around you and saying, 'I wish I had spent more time with them. They're what made my world go around.' If Verity wants to focus on that, and focus on a relationship and a family one day instead of a career, then we need to respect her choices."

"But—"

"Just be careful, Ella. You don't want to become like your mother."

Like her mother? "What do you mean?"

"Sometimes I worry that you are too scared to love, too scared of getting hurt, so you push people away like she did. Disengaging emotionally is not the answer."

Ella reeled back. "My mother wasn't like that." Dad, on the other hand …

Dad looked at her. "I mean your stepmother."

Ella stared at him, speechless. How could he have forgotten so quickly that *she* was the one who had always said she wanted a husband and family? Worse, how could he accuse her of being like her stepmother? Being told she was like the woman who had left Dad and Verity for a career was the ultimate insult. He might as well have slapped her. No, the pain went deeper than that. It was a betrayal, a degrading of who she was and all she stood for. The sooner she left home the better.

The very next day Ella applied to change her course to a Bachelor of Fine Arts and sent off a portfolio of all her best sketches. Doing so left her feeling strangely free. Who knew, she might even become a forensic sketch artist one day. She'd once watched a documentary about it, and the idea fascinated her. Helping the police with identifying suspects, helping bring closure to the lost and the hurting. It was probably beyond her, but it felt good to have a dream of her own. A dream that would take her far away from Morley and her past failures.

She would be a failure no more. She would push hard and push on every door available to see which one opened. But no way was she going to tell Verity her plans.

That evening she searched online for jobs in Sydney, close to the Uni. Any job would do. She didn't mind working in McDonald's. So long as she was far away from home and far away from Gabe and Verity.

Verity. Ella's fingers clenched. Who would have imagined she'd meet Gabe and change so drastically? It was as though she'd become a different person.

As though she'd become Ella.

***

The night before Ella left for her new life in Sydney, she glanced into Verity's room. Her sister lay on the bed, looking at her phone screen. A barrier had come between them. They were still civil to one another, but the closeness they'd shared as children was gone. Ella knew why. Verity's happiness was no longer something she took responsibility for. In fact, now Verity was something Ella had once vowed she would never let her sister become.

Her competition.

Regret squeezed her heart. How had it come to this? She felt trapped, confused. Maybe getting away would give her the chance to clear her head. "Knock, knock."

Verity looked up from her phone and smiled. "All ready to leave, hey?"

Ella nodded. She'd told Dad and Verity she had a job at McDonald's and would work there until her course began. She didn't tell them she'd changed preferences and that she'd now been accepted into a Bachelor of Fine Arts.

"What are you up to?" Ella asked. Verity still had a month before she began her course in Melbourne and she spent every moment she could with Gabe.

Verity tucked her phone away. "Nothing."

Ella shrugged. Fine. Shut her out. Then she glanced at Verity's bedside table. Alarm pulsed through her. "A baby magazine?"

Verity snatched it away.

"You've got to be kidding. Are you ... you're not pregnant?"

"No." Verity rolled her eyes. "I'm just planning for the future."

Ella sat on the end of Verity's bed, sadness welling up within. "Are you really going to throw away all your dreams, your future, all you've ever wanted for a boy—"

"He's not a boy. Gabe is a man."

"He's only just out of school. He's immature. He doesn't even know what he wants."

Verity sat up straight and her eyes flashed. "What's your problem? You can't have Gabe, so no one can?"

Should she tell her? Nothing else had worked. Ella drew in a deep breath. "Vee, that day Gabe first met you? He kissed me. Not even two hours before he came in and started making eyes at you, he kissed *me*."

Verity made a scoffing noise. "You think he didn't tell me? He was curious, Ella. He wanted to see how you'd react. And he told me exactly how you responded. He realised you're not ready for a relationship. There was zero chemistry there."

Hurt ripped through Ella's chest. Gabe had said that? She opened her mouth to respond, but nothing came out.

Verity let out a frustrated noise and threw down the magazine. "Look, I don't know why you're trying so hard to break us up, but I'm tired of this victim role you're playing. I'm tired of the way you pretend to be looking out for me, when the truth is, you can't stand for anyone else to be happy or know what they want because you don't know what *you* want."

Now that was going too far. Anger burned hot and red in Ella's chest at the injustice of it. "You think I don't know what I want? Well, let me tell you something. For as long as I remember, I've known what I wanted, but I sacrificed everything for *you*. But you know what? I'm tired of making way for your little whims just to keep you happy. If I said I wanted to go to the North Pole, you'd make sure you got there first. How about you think for yourself for a change? Forget about me. Forget about winning, about whatever this little game you play is. You have no right to mess with peoples' lives. If you hurt Gabe ..." She couldn't go on.

Verity's eyes widened. "You *do* have feelings for Gabe. That's why you're so upset about this." Her eyes filled with pity and her voice turned sweet. "Don't worry El. There will be someone for you too, someday. And they'll accept you just the way you are, and love you just the way you are."

Could she be any more patronising? An image of Monica flashed through Ella's mind. Telling her she was plain, that she needed to make sure Verity had what she wanted. Ella had stepped into the background for Verity. She saw that now. She'd wanted Verity to have the very best. Instead, her sister had become un-grateful, selfish, pushing others aside to get her own way.

"Oh El, I don't want to fight with you. Let's just accept that it's time to move on and live our own lives, shall we?" Verity came over and gave her a hug.

While Ella's heart broke into a thousand pieces.

Chapter Twelve

Two months later, Ella leaned back in the terrace deck chair, looking out into the night. City lights were much brighter than stars. Too bright. She missed the quiet of home. The Uni apartments were noisy until this time of night when curfew stated everyone should keep the noise down.

She closed her eyes, needing space to think. To feel. Someone had placed an Easter banner in the shared community room on her floor. A beautiful image of an old wooden cross on a hillside and an empty tomb with the stone rolled away. Splashed across the image were the words, 'He is Risen.'

For days the grammar had annoyed her. She knew it was something about Jesus, but shouldn't it say 'He has Risen'?

Everyone knew Nyree Wallace, a theology student, had put it there. Nyree talked about God as though He was real and with her every moment of the day. If Ella was honest, it freaked her out a bit. But tonight when Nyree was cooking her dinner in the community kitchen, Ella had finally found the courage to ask her about the banner.

"Yeah, it's from the old English version of the Bible." Nyree said, turning from the onion she was dicing. "Modern ones say 'He *has* Risen'. At first I looked everywhere for a banner with modern phrasing, but then I realised that saying He *is* risen makes it present tense. Like now. And Jesus is alive now. Here with us always, just waiting for us to reach out and talk to Him. I love that." She sniffed and wiped at her eyes. Ella couldn't tell from her voice if she was emotional or it was just the onions.

"So you can't get them with the modern phrasing on them?"

"No, they all use the old English. I think it's because there's no copyright on the old King James Version of the Bible." Nyree shook her head and tipped the chopped onion into the frying pan. "I don't know why people think they have the right to copyright a book written by God."

Nyree thought God wrote the Bible? Ella tried to keep the scepticism from her expression, but Nyree was observant.

"I mean that God inspired the Bible," Nyree said. "He got all different people throughout history to write about Him, about His words, His actions and interactions with people. The Bible actually has about thirty-five to forty different authors, all over about 1,500 years. And it all points to Jesus. I don't believe so many different authors over so many centuries could've put together such a powerful, inspirational historical book that fits together so perfectly without supernatural help."

"What do you mean it all points to Jesus?" Ella asked the question before she could second-guess herself.

Nyree pointed the knife in her hand toward the banner. "The people in the Old Testament were looking for a Saviour. Someone to mend the rift between wayward humans and a perfect God. God had promised a Saviour. That's Jesus. He sacrificed Himself out of love for us so that we can connect with Him, be made one with Him spiritually, and have all our sins paid for. Today, in our part of history, we look back at what He's done and trust in Him to forgive us and cleanse us from sin. All we have to do is accept and believe.

Then we become not only His friends but His adopted children. We are part of His family."

Ella frowned now, remembering Nyree's words. Sacrifice? She'd sacrificed herself her whole life for Verity's happiness. What a waste that had been. No more. Sacrificing your life for someone else wasn't worth it. She'd learned that the hard way.

The sliding door swished open behind her.

"What are you doing out here?" Brenton Tilbrook settled into the deck chair beside her.

Ella stiffened, then tried to relax. Brenton was doing the same Fine Arts course she was. He was harmless.

"Missing the stars. You could see them so clearly back home."

Brenton looked up into the sky. "Have you ever seen a shooting star?"

Memories flashed and her chest tightened. "Once." When she'd been sitting on the back verandah talking with Gabe.

"I haven't. I want to, though."

"What about a comet? I hear you can sign up to join the Halley's Comet viewing party in 2061."

Brenton laughed. "No way."

"You can." She pulled out her phone and showed him.

"Are you going?"

"No." Gabe would no doubt be there. Snuggled in a warm blanket with Verity by his side.

"Why not?"

"It'll be too cold." Same excuse she'd given Gabe.

Brenton laughed. "Oh, you're such a party pooper. The event information says to bring a blanket. And all your friends and family."

Ha. All her friends and family. She didn't have any. Not anymore. She resented the phone calls from Verity in Melbourne. Verity's monologue centred around 'Gabe did this; Gabe said that', as though the argument between them had never happened. Her sister was clearly obsessed with Gabe and couldn't see anyone or anything else.

Oh well. It just showed how lucky Ella was not to have fallen into the role of a devoted girlfriend, fiancée, or wife. Poor Gabe. How much was he having to sacrifice to make Verity happy? Would Verity take what she wanted from him and then abandon him, like she had with Ella?

If only she could remain angry at her sister, but she would always be in her heart. She was her family, her only sibling and she loved her. She'd fought for her happiness from the day she was born. Disappointed and hurt were better words for what she felt toward Verity now.

The way God feels about those who don't understand or accept His sacrifice.

Her skin prickled. Where had that thought come from?

Something stirred within. A memory. Sitting on the back verandah at home, looking out at the stars. That quiet voice of love and encouragement.

It must be God. It had to be.

The God that Nyree said wanted to be her friend. Her family. Maybe she should sign up to that crazy Halley's Comet Viewing Party and if no friends or family came, she'd sit and enjoy it with God. The way she'd enjoyed watching the stars with Him for years. She was willing, but would He come to the party? She wasn't so sure.

Chapter Thirteen

Ella lay on the bed in her small room and looked up at the ceiling. Someone had stuck glow-in-the dark balloon stickers around the light. She frowned as a memory resurfaced.

They'd been at the local fair and Dad bought both her and three-year-old Verity a helium balloon. Verity chose pink and Ella chose purple. Within two minutes, Verity became distracted by a clown riding past on a unicycle and her chubby little hand let go of her balloon. She'd wailed so loudly that even the clown had turned back to see what was wrong. Ella had loved her purple balloon, but she'd handed it over to Verity, unable to bear her sister's distress. Verity's little face had lit into a warm smile. But then she'd spotted another girl with a pink balloon like the one she'd lost. Screaming, she'd thrown the purple balloon in anger, and Ella had watched it sail up into the sky, far out of reach.

So many similar memories were buried in the back of Ella's mind. Each incident hadn't bothered her at the time. She'd believed it was worth it to keep Verity happy. But now she knew that Verity would only be happy if Ella was unhappy. And that was no longer a sacrifice she was willing to make.

Ella pulled out her pencils. Sketching happy faces made her happy and nothing was going to stop her doing that. She thought of each of the people in her accommodation building. She'd bring them joy by sketching them at their absolute best: smiling, laughing, relaxed. Then she'd place the portraits under each of their doors.

Her phone rang. She snatched it up, checking it wasn't Verity. She'd deleted that ridiculous ringtone of Verity's demanding voice months ago, but it also meant she had no warning that it was her sister calling until she'd look at her phone. Maybe she should change the ringtone for Verity to the Jaws theme.

This time Dad's name lit up her screen. She breathed a sigh of relief, unable to stomach the thought of speaking to Verity right now.

"Dad! It's so good to talk to you."

"Ella." He paused.

"How are you?" she prompted.

"Yeah, I'm good. How ... how is Sydney treating you?"

"Great. I'm still passing all my classes. Doing well."

"That's great." Another pause. "I have some news for you."

Ella held her breath. Was it about Verity and Gabe? If it was, she didn't want to hear it.

"Do you remember Barb Pilgrim who used to be the local florist?"

"Yeah, you built a deck for her a few years ago." Did he think she forgot everyone and everything back home when she left? Ella was the one who'd been home while Verity lived out her so-called dream of going to boarding school. She bit her lip, not liking the resentment searing her thoughts.

"Well," he cleared his throat, "She's moving in with me."

Shock splashed over Ella like a bucket of cold water. "Okay..." What else was there to say?

"She's good company," Dad was speaking fast now, "and as you've now found your niche in the city and Verity's moving to the States, I felt it was time to find my own life. And it saves on living expenses."

So what he had with them wasn't a life. So much for family being so important, and—

Wait. "Verity's going to the States?"

"Yes. She said she's been trying to call you but you must have blocked her."

"I haven't blocked her." Just ignored her.

"Well, it might be worth giving her a call. I'm a bit worried about her, and you've always been able to get through to her."

No. No way. She was not going to be the parent again. Not going to make sure Verity was happy. But then a thought struck. Verity wasn't going to the States to be with her mother, was she? Surely not. Worry churned in her stomach. What about her course in Melbourne? And what about Gabe?

Dad ended the call, like he'd said the hard stuff and cut the cord, as if he had already moved on. Her heart hurt. So much for family being forever. With shaking fingers, she called Verity, annoyed with herself that she couldn't leave well enough alone.

"Finally! You've got no idea how worried I've been, Ella," Verity said without even a hello. "I've been trying to contact you for ages. I thought something terrible must have happened to you."

"I've been busy. Dad says you're moving to the States."

"Yes, oh you're not going to believe it El, It's so exciting," Verity gushed. "Gabe's got a scholarship and I've got a traineeship."

"Gabe's going too?"

"Of course we're going together. We're in love, Ella."

"But what about your courses in Melbourne?"

"This is going to be so much better. I finally get to live out my dreams."

"Which dreams exactly?" Verity had waltzed from dream to dream so often over the years that Ella couldn't keep up anymore.

"Not saying."

"Why?"

"We have our different paths now, El. You can keep doing fashion and design. I'm not going to compete with you. The less you know, the better."

Was she for real? Sometimes Ella wondered if she was losing her mind. Verity was so good at twisting the truth, at turning everything back onto others, blame-shifting, gas-lighting, whatever you wanted to call it.

But with Dad living with Barb Pilgrim, moving on with her like his own daughters didn't matter, Verity was all the family Ella had left. She couldn't lose her, too. Why America? Unless... Her stomach twisted. Was Monica behind all of this?

"Can't Gabe keep studying in Australia? What's wrong with the business courses here?"

Verity let out a loud, overly-patient-sounding sigh as though trying to explain something to a small child. "Oh Ella, this is his chance to make it big. When he finishes this course, there's already a job lined up for him."

"Who set up the job for him? Not Monica?"

A loud scoffing noise came over the phone. "You think Gabe needs her help? He's smart enough to work his way to the top on his own. He was born to make a difference and I know he will. This job opportunity is more than he'd ever hoped for."

"So he's the one who wanted to go to the US? Or are you just pressuring him to follow your dreams?"

"Excuse me?" All sweetness drained from Verity's tone. "What are you implying? Gabe and I are in this together. We love each other. Just because you threw away what we have doesn't mean it's not worth having, Gabriella Glade!"

"Vee, I don't want to fight with you." Ella's throat burned. "You're all I have, really. Life has its funny twists and turns, but I don't want them to tear us apart."

Silence. Ella looked at her phone. Verity had ended the call. Well, if Verity was going to be like that, Ella was done. For good. If Verity wanted to call Ella would answer, but if not, she was finished reaching out, finished being hurt, finished giving and getting nothing in return. Verity was on her own.

***

After hearing nothing from Verity for two whole years, Ella called, only to find her number had been blocked. Concern warred with indignation. What was her sister doing? She called Dad.

"I don't hear from her either," Dad said. "She told me it costs too much to keep in touch from the States, and she never answers when I call."

Dad had probably been blocked too.

"Do you think she's okay?"

"Well, I see Margo Vance down the street sometimes. She still talks to Gabe and she said that Gabe assures her they're doing well."

Ella swallowed the lump in her throat. "Dad, why do you think Verity did this? Why has she cut us off this way?"

Dad was silent for a long moment. "She's like her mother, Ella. I wish I'd realised it sooner. I believe they both have a personality disorder. Their impulsivity, their need for attention, to be the hero in everybody's story, the way they live in their own reality and create their own narrative, twisting it to suit themselves." He sighed. "It's Margo Vance who brought it to my attention. She loves Verity, she really does. She's praying for her and doing her best to support Gabe so he can support and help Verity the best he can."

Ella's heart sank. She'd always hoped Verity would change as she matured, but was it possible? Could people with a personality disorder recover? Or was it just the way they were?

"She believes Verity and Gabe may have gotten married," Dad said.

"What?" Her chest grew tight. "Without telling us? Without inviting us?"

"Gabe mentioned something about eloping. Or Las Vegas. I don't know. Apparently Verity didn't want us there, believes we held her back, ruined her life."

Ella gasped. A knife slashing across her heart couldn't hurt more. No wonder Verity had cut them off. She was living out her own lies and didn't want anyone to stumble on her family or the truth.

Fine. Let Verity be that way. She, Gabriella Glade, would continue with her own life and put her sister out of her mind. She loved her studies, loved art, and now dreamed of being a criminal sketch artist. She might be a bit incompetent in everyday life, but when she was drawing she felt alive.

And it was time to truly live.

PART TWO

Chapter Fourteen

TEN YEARS LATER ...

Ella sat, pencil poised as the witness tried to describe what she remembered of the suspect.

"Um, he had longish hair."

"To his shoulders?"

"No, no," the woman shook her head. "More like it just needed a trim."

"Like this?" Ella sketched lines across the face shape she'd already determined from the woman's memory, adding in wispy, unkempt hair.

"Yes. Yes, that's right."

"What about his nose? Do you remember the shape of his nose?"

The woman frowned. "Well, I do, but I don't know how to describe it."

Ella opened the folder containing different facial features and flipped to the noses. "Can you see one in here that might be similar?"

"Um ..." The woman frowned and Ella saw the sweat beading on her forehead.

"It's okay, Mrs. Cole. You won't be in trouble if you get it wrong. This is just to give us an idea. Even a guess will help."

As always, her reassurance helped. Mrs. Cole's shoulders relaxed and her forehead smoothed. She rattled off features in steady succession, working with Ella who adjusted until Mrs. Cole was satisfied they'd captured an image of the man they were looking for.

"It's incredible," Mrs. Cole breathed in wonder as she studied the sketch. "It's him. It's really him. How did you do that?"

Ella smiled. "I couldn't have done it without you. You've been an amazing witness. Thank you."

Detective Cooper led the woman from the room and Ella went back to her desk to scan in her copy of the sketch. She didn't like working digitally, so Detective Cooper insisted she copy her sketches onto the computer as soon as she'd finished them. She hoped the man was found. She was never given details of the cases, but she knew this man was suspected of murder. Mrs. Cole had clearly been shaken and Ella was glad her job didn't involve hearing all the details. It was the perfect job, really. Helping find criminals without having to hear the horrific details of their crime.

Her phone rang. She glanced at the number. Unfamiliar. She declined the call. It rang again. She put it on silent and reached for the sketch.

Where was it? How could she lose one lousy sketch the moment she'd finished it? She searched through the papers on her desk. She was a professional, and one of the country's most sought-after forensic sketch artists. Surely she should have grown out of her haphazard ways by now?

This was the very reason Detective Cooper kept pushing her to use technology for her sketches, but she couldn't get the hang of using a stylus pen. None had the same feel as pencil on paper, and she needed that to be able to think.

"Ella?"

Tait Ellison, her co-worker, held out his hand, waiting for the sketch. He had that knowing look on his face that she'd grown used to. His intelligent eyes seemed to read her every thought. Some days it made her nervous.

"Oh, um, sorry. I had it here just a second ago."

Tait appeared as patient as ever, but she knew he needed the sketch as soon as possible. Time was of the essence in murder cases. Now she'd done the sketch, it was Tait's turn. If anyone could identify and find this criminal, Tait could. He was amazing, the way his mind worked. Nothing went missing on his watch. He noticed everything, including every nuance of body language. Then he'd put it all together, never missing even the smallest detail. He was a genius.

"Tait is not your everyday police officer," Detective Cooper had said when he'd first introduced their new team member two years ago. "He was once a black hat hacker but he's now in witness protection and using his skills to help us out. He's not only a tech expert, but he's brilliant at reading people. We're just glad he's now on our side."

She'd been doubtful at first. Especially when she'd discovered Tait's real name was Tanner Elliott, with a brother, Joel, who was a convicted con-man and murderer.

But Tanner, or Tait as they knew him, had proved himself time and time again. He'd even told her what had changed him. An encounter with God. Ella sometimes wondered if God was trying to tell her something. Surely it couldn't be a coincidence how many Christians appeared down every path she took in life?

Tait's lips lifted as she scrabbled through more papers. He nodded toward the mess scattered across her desk. "Mind if I have a look?"

"Not at all." She slid her chair back and watched as he flipped through the items. Then he looked beneath the desk.

"Here." He picked up a piece of paper from the floor and turned it over. She sighed with relief to see her sketch, but Tait frowned as he studied it.

"Is there any way you can add a beard? Maybe some age lines? I just have a feeling ..."

A feeling for Tait usually meant he actually did know something. That he'd observed, calculated, worked out something important.

"Like this?" She grabbed another sheet of paper and copied her sketch before adding the beard and age lines. Memories flashed and her hand faltered.

"What's wrong?" Tait never missed a thing.

"Nothing. Just a memory."

His intelligent eyes studied her. "To do with this case?"

"No. A memory from the past." Of adding the same features to the newspaper photo of Gabriel Vance all those years ago. She remembered how he'd looked at her in that amused way of his when he'd realised what she'd done.

"Remember I'm your dream future husband," Gabe would sometimes say, just to embarrass her.

"I only thought that because I hadn't met you in person yet," she'd retort.

"Oh, come on, you know you want to marry me."

And perhaps she had wanted to, deep down.

But then he'd met Verity. Verity who'd always wanted whatever Ella had.

They had a daughter now, or so Dad's annual Christmas card had informed her. She suspected by the writing that Barb was the one who wrote the cards each year, but at least someone had bothered to tell her. Gabe and Verity named their daughter Lacy, the card had said. The little girl would be two years old now. Ella had yet to meet her, but she'd sent a gift for Dad to pass on to her niece. She'd chosen a pink teddy bear with a sweet face and huge brown eyes. Like Gabe's. She tried not to wonder if her niece had eyes like Gabe's, a smile like his. She couldn't wait to meet the little girl. One day soon she'd make a surprise trip to the States. She'd ask Gabe's mother for Verity's address and ask her to keep the trip a secret. Hopefully Gabe and Verity would welcome her. They should have room for her, because she'd also heard via the Christmas card that Gabe had sold a business plan he'd created and now had more money than he knew what to do with. He'd always been smart. Ironically, he was now the rich man she'd imagined him to be when she'd first sketched him.

But she sure hadn't imagined him married to her sister while she, Ella, worked her way up in her career to become a successful forensic sketch artist.

Funny how the world turned.

"Tait. Ella. I need you in my office. Now."

Ella glanced at Tait. Detective Cooper didn't sound happy. Had she taken too long on the sketch? Taking the sketch with them, Tait and Ella entered Detective Cooper's office.

He looked up from his desk, expression serious. "Close the door."

Tait closed the door while Detective Cooper indicated they should both sit down. His laptop was open on his desk. Ella searched his face for any clue as to why they'd been called in. He held out his hand for Ella's sketch and then placed it on the desk in front of her.

"Does the suspect look familiar to you?"

"To me?" She was surprised by the question. "No, why?"

"Are you sure?"

Ella glanced nervously at Tait, then back to the detective. "I'm sure. I remember faces, and I've never seen him before. Why?"

"We believe this man is Orson Carnegie. He's the managing partner of a large and very successful real estate business in the US. One the US police have been investigating for several months now."

Ella's ears pricked up. "Investigating for what?" She wasn't usually given details of cases.

"Carnegie's business partner reported him of suspected criminal activity. Some things were not adding up. And now the partner's fiancée appears to have been murdered."

Ella frowned. What did this all have to do with her? Detective Cooper was looking at her as though something should be clicking into place in her mind.

"So why are we investigating if this is a US company?"

"The victim died on a plane in Australian air space and she is a dual Australian/US citizen." He tilted his head. "Ella, we have just been given contact details for the victim's family. Your name was on that list."

"What?" She jerked back. Surely she hadn't heard him right? "Who is the victim?"

"Verity Langley-Moore."

The blood froze in Ella's veins. Nausea swirled in her stomach. It couldn't be. "I ... I do have a sister named Verity, but her last name is Vance. And she's married. She's not some real-estate man's fiancée. She can't be the same Verity." She heard the panic in her own voice.

Detective Cooper spun his laptop around to show her two images on his screen.

One of Verity.

One of Verity's mother, Monica Langley-Moore.

And Ella knew her world had just been turned upside down.

Dread settled in her stomach. Breath constricted in her lungs.

"You recognise them?" Detective Cooper prompted.

"My step-mother," she whispered, pointing a shaking finger at the picture of Monica Langley-Moore. Why did her heart still jar at the sight of the woman? She was long gone. She had no power over her anymore.

"And this one?"

"That's my sister." She looked at Detective Cooper, clinging to a tiny strand of hope. Now was his turn to admit they'd made a mistake. Her sister was not the victim. It was someone else, who by some coincidence had the same first name. "Her name is Verity Vance."

Detective Cooper shook his head. "I'm sorry, Ella. She goes by Verity Langley-Moore."

Ella blinked hard. "No, she married Gabe Vance. Ten years ago. They have a daughter. Before that she was Verity Glade."

"Ella." Compassion shone from Detective Cooper's eyes as he pointed to the photo of Verity. "Gabriel Vance of Carnegie & Vance Real Estate is her fiancé, and this woman, your stepsister, Verity Langley-Moore, is deceased."

His words were like a blow to the stomach. Nausea swirled. How could he be so blunt? So cold? She closed her eyes, warding off the dizziness threatening to overwhelm her. "What happened to her?" she whispered. She needed something to ground her. Something that made sense to hold onto.

Detective Cooper waited until she looked up at him again. "She was on a plane from the US to Australia when she went into cardiac arrest. It appears she was drinking tea containing lethal amounts of arnica."

"Arnica?" Ella blinked, as thoughts raced around her head. She dug her fingernails into her leg but felt nothing. Everything was numb.

"It's a flowering herb. Some people use it on their skin as a herbal remedy for bruising, others drink it in their tea in low doses. Your sister was drinking from a water bottle filled with arnica tea, but excessive amounts had been added. She told the lady in the seat beside her it was good for preventing deep vein thrombosis on long flights."

Deep vein thrombosis. What Ella's mother had died of. Her heart thudded.

"So what makes you think she was murdered? Couldn't she have accidentally had too much?"

Detective Cooper shook his head. "We don't think so. Airport cameras show a man handing her the water bottle with the tea in it. He's facing away from the camera, but the man you just sketched gave her the bottle. He's our main suspect."

Ella's eyes filled. "I don't understand."

"We'll find who did this and why, Ella," Detective Cooper assured her. "Tait's on it already."

Ella's head swam. Detective Cooper was watching her every move, almost as though he were gauging her reaction. Was she a suspect too? He pulled out a notepad and pen.

"Did your sister tell you she was coming to visit? Coming to Australia?"

"No." Ella's swallowed hard. "We didn't keep in touch."

"But you said your sister was married to Gabriel Vance. Do you have any evidence of that?"

"Just what I was told." But now she didn't know what to believe. Confusion weighed down her shoulders like a heavy cloak, covering the truth she was so desperately searching for.

"And you haven't heard of Carnegie & Vance Real Estate in Georgia?"

"No," her voice was small, "but we kind of led separate lives once Verity left for the States with Gabe."

Detective Cooper frowned. "I need you to start from the beginning. Tell me your understanding of your sister's connection to Gabriel."

As Ella related the way Verity had fallen for Gabe then left for the States, Detective Cooper's frown grew.

"They said Gabe received a scholarship into a business school over there," Ella said. "So it made sense when Gabe's mum said he made lots of money from a business model he came up with. I didn't know anything about a real estate company."

"And you were told Gabe is Lacy's father."

"Yes." She saw the look on his face. "But there's no *way* he would've poisoned Verity."

The detective's serious gaze met hers. "Sometimes what we think we know about people simply isn't true."

Wasn't that the truth? If Gabe and Verity hadn't really married—had Verity been lying all this time? And what about Lacy? Was she even real, or was she make-believe, much like Verity's marriage to Gabe seemed to have been?

Surely Ella hadn't been loving a little girl who didn't exist all this time, dreaming of the day she'd finally meet her?

Ella swallowed, managed to speak. "So what now?"

"We're following up all leads. Your niece was on the plane with her mother and she's been taken into protective custody."

Air filled her lungs. "So Lacy does exist?"

"Yes, she exists. And interestingly, although there's no record of a marriage between Gabriel Vance and Verity Lang-ley-Moore, Lacy's surname is Vance."

"Can I see Lacy?" Her chin trembled and Detective Cooper tilted his head to the side.

"No, I'm sorry, Ella. At least not yet."

"But the poor little girl probably doesn't understand what's happening. She must be so frightened."

Detective Cooper didn't budge. "She's being taken good care of. And from what you've said, she doesn't know you."

It was true. Ella stood, rubbing her hands down her face. The heavy lump in her throat said she needed to cry, but her mind was racing, unable to land in a safe place. She needed to work this all out. Lacy had Gabe's last name, and yet Verity supposedly wasn't married to him? She stood and paced the room.

"Why has Lacy been taken into protective custody?"

"I can't tell you at this point."

Frustration at the lack of answers fuelled a groan. Was it possible Verity was killed to get to Lacy? Was someone trying to abduct the little girl and claim a ransom from Gabe? His mother had said he was rich. Exactly how rich was he?

She stopped pacing. "Where's Gabe?"

"On his way over in one of his company's planes. He'll be with Lacy as soon as he can be."

Well, that answered the question about how rich he was. But if an abductor managed to kill Verity, why didn't they take Lacy? "You realise none of this makes sense? My head feels like it's going to explode. I can't even think right now."

"You don't have to." Detective Cooper's face held compassion. "This is one case you're no longer involved in. We'll find another sketch artist and Tait will help us find our suspect. And you are going to keep a low profile and have some time off until we figure this out."

Ella felt panic setting in. She needed to work on the case. Otherwise this would overwhelm her. Drown her. She'd learned from the day she left home that if she wanted to survive and not be dragged down by her thoughts and lost in her own head, then she needed to be busy. That was how she'd managed to top her class in fine arts, to receive an offer of placement to study criminology. She mightn't have Gabe and Verity's talent, but she knew the value of pure, hard work.

"Please." She tried not to sound as desperate as she felt. "I need to work on this. I'll be safe here. Tait's in witness protection and he's safe here."

"You're too close to this, Ella." His expression softened. "Trust us. Trust the system. We'll get this sorted and have our murderer behind bars as soon as possible."

Ella's chest tightened as reality began to set in. Verity was gone. It felt surreal. "Are you sure it's Verity? Has someone identified her?"

"We will ask your father to."

"What about a funeral? For Verity?"

"It'll have to wait. I'm sorry, but we need people to think she survived this. At least until we solve the case."

Everything about this was so very wrong. Verity, the one who was born to stand out, who liked to be noticed, to have the spotlight on her, was leaving this world without any recognition at all.

Except for the lonely anguish of a grieving sister who wasn't even allowed to help find her killer.

Chapter Fifteen

Tait drove Ella home. Detective Cooper insisted, saying it would be negligent to let her drive while she was still in shock.

"I'm so sorry this has happened," Tait said as he indicated and slowed to turn into her driveway. "But I promise you, I'll put everything I have into seeking justice for your sister."

She nodded, unable to find the words to thank him. She felt numb. Lost.

He pulled up in the driveway and she fumbled with the door handle, needing to escape the closed-in feel of his vehicle. Out of habit she stopped at her mailbox, pulled out a package and turned it over. She froze. From Verity? Reason warred with hope. She'd never received anything from Verity. Ever. And yet Verity was gone. Wasn't she? Was this sent before she died?

"Tait?"

Tait moved to her side and glanced at the sender's address. He turned it over.

"Don't move." His voice was low and urgent. In one smooth transition, he slid the package from her hands and lowered it to the ground. "Quick. Get back in the car."

His tone scared her. Every nerve was on edge as she dived back into the passenger side of the car and slammed the door.

Tait threw the car into gear and roared out of the driveway.

"Tait, what's going on?" Her voice shook.

"That package is not from Verity. The mail stamps are fake. Someone hand-delivered it and I know it wasn't Verity. They might be watching the place now." He pressed speed-dial on his dashboard display unit. "Detective? You need to send a team to Ella's house. We've left a package on the ground near her mailbox. It says it's from Verity."

"On it."

Detective Cooper's urgent tone and abrupt end to the call made her more nervous. She looked over at Tait. "What do you think is in it?"

"I wouldn't even try to guess." Tait glanced at her as they came around the corner, back to work. "We'll let the forensics tell us that, but it's possible someone's trying to harm you."

"What do I do now?"

"Stay with me until our team have inspected the package and gone through your home."

She winced at the thought of them going through her personal belongings. Was it really necessary?

For a tense five hours, Ella sat at her desk — the safest place for her, Detective Cooper had said — and tried to process what was happening. Her mind tumbled over, switching between questions, memories and grief. Funny how all the good memories of Verity assailed her now, after years of living and re-living the bad ones. There had been good times. Like the time they'd made a cubby house using the dining room table and chairs and some old bedsheets. Dad had let them sleep under there and they'd talked and giggled for hours before finally falling asleep.

And the time Ella had pneumonia when she was ten years old. She'd been coughing through the night and Verity had come in, worry in her eyes, asking if there was anything she could do. Verity had brought her another blanket and a drink of water, then slept beside her all night. She'd been warm and comforting and Ella had known she was loved.

Yes, there had been good times. Why had it been so easy to focus on the bad and hold on to her anger these past ten years? It hurt that the last time she'd spoken to Verity, their words to each other had been harsh and bitter. If only she'd known what the future held …

Finally, Detective Cooper called Ella into his office. The parcel held some packets of arnica tea that appeared to have been tampered with and added to, he told her. And with them was a typed letter supposedly from Verity, telling Ella she'd discovered the benefits of arnica tea for those who had a genetic pre-disposition to blood clots. She encouraged Ella to try it, especially if she planned to fly anywhere. She then mentioned a possible surprise visit to Ella at some stage. However, the wording of the letter was stilted, unlike Verity's writing, and had no fingerprints attached.

"I think someone's trying to get you to go the same way Verity did," Detective Cooper said.

Breath hitched. "But why? That's absurd, unbelievable."

"Your sister's death is all too real. And if they know where you live and are trying to hurt you, then we need to take you into protective custody."

***

Ella lay awake in a strange motel room with security at her door. Tears kept sliding from her eyes, but she refused to make a sound. Her body shook with the effort of holding them back. If only she could be alone and release the cries of anguish building up deep inside, screaming to be set free. If only she could wake from this awful nightmare called life.

She thought of Gabe, then his mother. How she wished Margo Vance was here. The one person who had ever shown her the compassion she yearned for as a girl. Margo would understand, would circle warm, motherly arms around her now, wrap a bandage around her heart and bind her wounds. Because this was the deepest pain, the most cutting devastation, the most confusing experience of her life. Falling during a race was nothing compared to having her sister gone from this life without so much as a goodbye or an explanation for the years of distance, for all the competition, for all the lies.

God? Are you there?

The silent, desperate cry came from somewhere deep within.

A knock came on her door. "Gabriella, we have your father on the phone."

Dad. She had nothing to say to him. Nothing with which to comfort him. Nothing to give.

The police officer passed through a phone. She'd had to surrender hers. She drew in a deep breath and forced herself to speak.

"Dad? Have you seen Verity? Is it true? Is it really true?"

"Oh, Ella." His voice was raspy and she knew he'd been crying. "Yes, it's our Verity." He drew in a shaky breath. "Are you okay?"

No. She doubted she'd ever be okay again. "I'm safe. How about you?"

"Safer than you it seems. I was told about the parcel you received. The police have warned me to be careful, but they don't think there's any threat to me at this stage."

"Dad, what do you think Vee got herself into?"

Her father let out a heavy sigh. "I have no idea."

"Detective Cooper said there's no record of her being married."

"I know."

"Why would she lie to us?"

"I hardly think that matters now."

But it did. If she was to understand any of this, she had to understand what had happened between Gabe and Verity. Ella's whole life had been impacted by their relationship, if there even was one. The choices she'd made, the hurts she'd had to battle, the facts she'd wrestled to come to terms with ...

If they weren't facts at all, then her whole world had been turned upside down again.

"When did you last speak to her, Dad?"

"Um, I don't remember."

"What did you talk about?" She had to know, had to grasp that last piece of the living Verity, that last connection.

"I'm sorry, I honestly can't remember. It didn't seem important. We have our own lives now, Ella. You with your work, me and Barb—"

"No, Dad! You have your own life. And Verity did too. But I don't. I still need my family. I don't have a new one."

Dad fell silent and Ella cringed. She hadn't meant to admit her vulnerability, her loneliness.

"Ella, I'm sorry."

She shook her head, trying to dislodge the guilt now filling her. Dad had just lost his daughter and she was putting this on him, too.

The silence stretched. Ella rubbed her burning eyes. "I wish I could see you, Dad. I wish I could be with you right now. I'm sorry I've been distant for so long."

"It's okay," Dad said. "Don't worry about me. You stay safe and take care of you. Barb and I have each other."

And she had no one.

Her sister, her closest childhood friend and later her greatest opposition, had died in the middle of nowhere, between the two countries she had lived in during her short life.

She choked on a sob. Was she the only one who truly felt the loss of Verity? The little girl who'd once shared a room with her in their small childhood home? The one who dressed up as a princess, who giggled with her late into the night, who shared her secret hopes and dreams? That was the Verity she was grieving. Not the teenage Verity who became dramatic, self-centred, and competitive. Not the sister who manipulated, used, and lied to her.

What had happened? What had changed Vee so much?

And why would she and Gabe pretend to be married? Ella looked down at her finger. The one that had caught in the ring binder fifteen years ago, the day she had met Gabe Vance. The pain hit her all over again. Only this time it wasn't a blood-blister forming on her finger. It was forming on her heart, pinching, squeezing, biting. A wound that would never heal.

Chapter Sixteen

Ella awoke to a knock on the door of her motel room. A voice came through.

"Ella? You awake?"

And it all came flooding back. She ignored the nausea roiling in her stomach and came to the door. She unlatched it and peeked through, breathing a sigh of relief to see Tait. She opened the door wider. "I am now. Any news? I just need to know what's going on."

"We're making progress."

"That's it?" Surely he could tell her something more?

"Detective Cooper will explain soon, but you need to get ready to leave again."

"What? Where am I going? I don't even have a change of clothes."

"Ella," Tait sounded weary. "You can trust Detective Cooper. You need to."

Trust. How could she trust when everything she'd believed for the past ten years was a lie? And yet, somehow, deep down, she knew Tait was trustworthy.

"I'll get ready."

It didn't take long to put together the few things she had with her. Detective Cooper handed her a muffin and a hot coffee the moment she opened the door again, before leading her to a black car with dark windows.

"You're going to be taken to a cottage in the country," he said. "Everything will be explained when you arrive."

Ella ran her hands over her face. With no phones, no technology, no one to talk to, no work to focus on, she might go insane.

As she was driven down unfamiliar, winding roads away from the city, she found herself silently talking to the God she hoped with all her heart was real.

I need your help, God. My head won't stop swimming. This is surreal. Like some movie, or some strange kind of joke. If it's you who's in charge of this crazy world, of everything that happens, then I need you to show me what all of this means. Show me what to do. I'm completely at your mercy.

Her prayer continued throughout the drive and by the time they turned down a dirt track out in the middle of nowhere, her tense muscles relaxed. What did she have to lose by living out here? Verity was gone and she clearly had no control over what happened in this world so she might as well surrender to it. Just like she'd surrendered to her step-mother's abuse as a child. Just like she'd surrendered to Verity's whims, to Dad's careless ways.

"Here we are." The driver pulled up in front of a small farm cottage. Further down the road Ella saw the tip of the roof of a much larger home.

She stepped from the car.

"Ella!" A woman rushed toward her, a little girl in her arms. Recognition dawned. Margo Vance, still poised and beautiful but now with grey hair and a few wrinkles.

Ella had been desperate for this woman's embrace only hours earlier, but now everything within her was drawn to the little girl in the pink dress who clung to Margo. Ella's heart swelled, captured by the cherubic face and the vulnerability in the little girl's eyes. Eyes so much like her own.

"Lacy?" she whispered.

Margo nodded. "Ella, meet Lacy."

At last. Her niece's tiny hands clutched a familiar pink teddy, now ragged and well-loved. So she had received it. Ella's chest constricted and she swallowed back a sob. The child reached out her free hand to Ella. The tiniest of smiles peeked through, revealing a dimple, then her eyes lit up and she dropped her teddy, both plump toddler arms reaching out to Ella, asking to be held.

Ella took her from Margo's arms and pulled her close, tears burning her throat as the little girl snuggled in and rested her tousled hair against her shoulder. She looked down into the beautiful, expressive face and knew that through her daughter, Verity lived on.

"Her eyes are just like yours," Margo's quiet voice said.

Ella drew in a shaky breath, unable to respond. She hadn't seen the woman in years, not since Verity and Gabe had left for Melbourne. How awful that it had taken the death of her sister to bring them together again.

Strangers surrounded them, most of them in dark suits and police uniforms. Some spoke into their phones, others kept a watchful eye on their surroundings.

Around her, American detectives spoke in brisk, commanding accents as they talked with their Australian counterparts. They looked out of place here on a small Australian farm and she hated the reason they were here. The States had stolen her sister from her. Stolen Verity's life, her joy, and her right to a fitting send off.

The anguish Ella felt threatened to overcome her, but she held it in and focused on Lacy. The niece she'd only just met, who'd found in her a friend and comforter. The toddler flashed another shy, uncertain smile. One that made Ella feel as though she were looking at a younger version of herself.

"Where's Mr. Vance?" Ella asked.

A shadow passed over Margo's face. "He passed away. Last year. A stroke."

"I'm so sorry." More death. More loss.

Another black car came down the road toward them. A man was escorted from the back seat. Margo let out a cry and ran to embrace him. Ella immediately knew who he was. Tall, dark, head down. A beard covered his face, but she'd recognise him anywhere. Gabriel Vance, the man who'd swept her sister off her feet and left with her for the States.

The man who was once her best friend.

Funny how things turned out. How the world turned. And right now, her world had been turned completely upside down.

She watched Gabe's every step as he came closer. He looked so much older. His dark brown gaze lifted and settled on his little girl. Her chest tensed as a soft expression passed through the grief etched in his eyes.

Lacy reached her arms out to him. "Daddy."

Ella passed her over, moved by the way the little girl clung to her father, then patted his cheeks.

"Wet," she said, "All wet."

Ella saw that indeed, tears were silently tracking down his cheeks. She swallowed and looked away, giving them privacy. Finally he lowered Lacy to the ground and Ella met his gaze.

"Ella." His voice was deeper than she remembered, his face more mature. Maybe it was the beard. His once carefree, boyish charm was gone, replaced by a maturity born of pain and loss.

"I'm so sorry," she whispered. "For everything. I'm sorry about Verity, sorry I didn't keep in touch …"

His glistening eyes fastened on hers. "Me too."

Years of friendship and understanding pooled in his gaze, and yet this man Gabe felt like a stranger. How could she ask all the questions that stood like a wall between them?

Feeling a gentle tug at her hand, she looked down at Lacy. Confusion filled those wide hazel eyes.

"Mommy?" Her American accent was strong.

Ella's chest felt tight. "No, little one. I'm Aunty Ella."

Lacy tilted her head then smiled, a hesitant, but very real smile. She lifted her arms up to be held and gently, Ella lifted her. The little girl wrapped her arms around her neck and clung on as though terrified she'd leave.

"You sound like Verity," Margo said softly. "And you have her smile."

Ella didn't respond. As lovely as the woman was, she wished she could send everyone away and be alone with Lacy, her Lacy. Fierce protectiveness rose up within, the same protectiveness she'd felt for Verity when they were little. But this time she wasn't helpless. She was strong. An adult. She could make choices. She could fight anything and anyone who tried to hurt Lacy. She gave Gabe's mother a slight nod, then turned her attention back to Lacy.

"I'm your mummy's sister." She knew the two-year-old wouldn't understand, but needed to speak the words. "She sounds like me, but we're different. Very different. Except that I love you like she did. I love you, Lacy."

Lacy held her tighter and placed a sloppy kiss on her nose. "Mommy?"

"I'm Aunty Ella."

"Mommy El?"

Ella looked helplessly at Margo.

"It's okay," Margo said quietly. "She knows you're not her mother, but she's been through so much trauma. It might help if you can fill the space of a mother for now."

Ella's chin quivered as she pulled Lacy closer. How was she ever going to let this little girl go?

All too soon, Gabe interrupted. "Lacy, let's go. These men need to speak with Ella."

"Mommy El?" Lacy's little finger pointed to Ella. Then she looked around. "Where's Mommy?

Ella drew in a deep breath. How would Gabe respond to that question?

He came and lifted Lacy into his arms. "I think I saw some cows. Do you want to see them?"

"Yes, Daddy, yes." Lacy bounced with excitement, her mother forgotten for the moment. Gabe lifted his daughter over his head to sit on his shoulders.

"We'll see you soon," Margo said and Ella blinked hard, watching them walk to the nearby fence.

It felt as though she was losing Verity all over again. She needed Lacy, and Lacy needed her. But what could she do about it? The frustration and helplessness made her want to lash out. She looked around at the men waiting to speak with her.

"You'll be staying here in the cottage," Detective Cooper said, taking the lead. "We'll have a security guard on the property, and we'll provide someone to go with you if you need to go anywhere."

He pointed to the large house. "Margo Vance will be living there, and Gabriel will come and go under police guard."

"Really? You're placing us together? I thought in these instances you separated acquaintances?"

"Sometimes we do, but in this case, Lacy's emotional stability was a determining factor. With additional security measures in place, we feel this is the best option for everyone."

"So will Lacy come and go with Gabe?" Lacy was the only one who mattered right now.

"No, she'll be with you."

That was a surprise. Ella breathed out a sigh of relief. She wouldn't have to fight for her niece. She could make sure she was safe.

"Where will Gabe be going?"

Detective Cooper glanced at his counterparts. One of them stepped forward and spoke. "He will be helping us with our investigations."

"So he's not a suspect?"

"No."

A weight lifted from her heart. Once she would never have believed Gabe of such a thing, but now her whole world had been turned upside down and she didn't know what to believe anymore.

A lady handed Ella a phone. She hadn't noticed her in amongst all the men. She was dressed exactly like them.

"I'm Nicola. If you need us, you can use this phone. Three numbers are programmed in. Me, Tait, and Margo. Other numbers are blocked for your own safety."

"What about my dad?"

"We understood you're not especially close." The lady's sympathetic expression softened her words. "We need to keep your contacts minimal for now, but he and his partner are safe."

Ella nodded. At least she still had contact with Tait. He was her closest friend these past few years, if she could call him a friend. More like a brother. He was the one person who knew everything about her, partly because he worked for the police, partly because he was observant, and partly because she'd needed someone to talk to. She trusted him, and now she understood some of what he was going through. Being in protective custody, having to trust someone else to protect you and losing your freedom for your own safety, was not an easy thing.

Especially when the reason was the death of a loved sister. Yes, Verity had been difficult and selfish, but Ella had loved her. Loved her still.

Chapter Seventeen

The cottage was delightful. Ella smiled at the toddler bed already set up in one room, covered with a purple blanket and almost hidden by an array of soft toys. Then she came to her room.

"We collected a few personal items including clothes from your flat," the uniformed lady said. Ella couldn't remember her name, but she nodded her thanks. She was still in her clothes from yesterday and couldn't wait to shower and change.

"We've filled the pantry and you're able to request anything else you want. Shopping, personal items, food ... Just let us know and someone will get it for you. However, Margo Vance said she'd be very happy to cook for you and Lacy."

Again, Ella nodded.

"I'll take you up to the main house and you can have a look around and reacquaint yourself with the Vance family."

Ella followed the lady outside. The security guard who'd been introduced as 'Savage' joined them as they walked up to the house. Ella knew it was his surname but couldn't hide her amusement. He looked serious and watchful like Tait, and maybe even a bit intimidating, but not savage.

The house was a beautiful building, possibly older than the cottage. It looked ageless, like a fortress protecting its occupants from the outside world. A wide verandah surrounded the house with vines running down one side.

Gabe was the first person Ella saw as she came in the door. He sat quietly in a large living room with a sleepy-looking Lacy snuggled against his chest. He looked down at his daughter with such affection that Ella found a lump forming in her throat. He was clearly a good father. Gabe looked up and again his eyes met hers. Something squeezed around Ella's heart as she allowed herself to fully study him. This Gabe with the manly beard that hid his smile was not the charming, mischievous teenager she'd once known. He wore a dark business suit rather than the casual clothes he had worn all those years ago when he'd dropped by her house to visit. He stood, still holding Lacy, and his walk was slow and heavy with no evidence remaining of his boyish, youthful enthusiasm.

"I'll just put her down for her nap," he said.

The now empty room was stifling. Ella could hear Savage speaking on the phone nearby, probably to an agent. The walls were closing in.

She escaped outside and sat on the edge of the verandah, letting her legs hang off the edge. She studied the hills. Verity was gone. It felt surreal. She looked up at the sky. Would the stars ever twinkle again? Nothing felt alive anymore. Not the scenery, not the world or her heart. Something inside felt as though it had shrivelled up and died. With a deep sigh she lowered her head into her hands. Then she heard footsteps along the verandah and a sigh deeper than her own.

Gabe.

He stopped when he saw her and seemed undecided for a moment. Then he lowered himself onto the verandah beside her, his long legs reaching the ground. He slipped off his suit jacket and set it neatly beside him. She waited for him to say something, but he didn't. She hated this silence, the reason for it. The loss of connection over so many years, and now the loss of Verity.

"I have so many questions, Gabe." She blurted it out before she could second-guess herself.

He turned and met her gaze, ran a hand down his beard. "I'll answer the ones I can."

"You didn't marry her?" It was hard to know where to start, but there was as good a place as any.

He visibly swallowed. "No."

"Why?"

"I planned to when we left for the US, but I needed to wait until she was eighteen. And then, well ..." He cleared his throat. "Our relationship became difficult. I wanted to come home, but I was obliged to stay."

"Why?"

"Monica and her partner had paid for my studies and I signed a contract to say I'd work in her partner's real estate firm for at least five years after I finished."

"Monica? Verity's mum?"

"Yeah. I made some foolish choices."

"So Monica convinced you both to go over there? I was told you had a scholarship. And then that you sold a business model for some huge amount of money."

"Yeah." He sighed. "Verity asked me to say I had a scholarship. She didn't want anyone knowing her mother was involved."

"So you lied for her?" She bit her tongue. Who was she to judge? She of all people understood how sweet and charming ... and manipulative Verity could be.

"I lied about the marriage." His dark eyes were filled with regret. "But I did actually create a business model which included a computer program for real estate clients. It made the process of choosing and buying a property so much simpler and kept track of all taxes, fees and costs involved. Unfortunately, Orson Carnegie claimed it was his intellectual property because he was paying for my studies. He did pay me a huge amount for it, and Monica made sure I knew how generous he was being, but in hindsight I believe it was to make sure I didn't challenge his rights to it."

"So he's making money from it and not compensating you?"

Gabe hesitated. "Actually, no. He hasn't used it at all."

"That doesn't make sense."

Again, that pause. Then, "My program would have showed clients when they were being ripped off."

"Oh." It all fell into place, and explained why Carnegie & Vance Real Estate was being investigated. Of course they wouldn't want people using a program that showed they were ripping off clients or stealing from them in some way. "Did ... did Carnegie threaten to hurt Verity to keep you quiet?"

"No." He rubbed a hand across his eyes and his shoulders sagged. "I'm sorry, but I'm not supposed to talk about the case. To anyone. I shouldn't have said as much as I have."

She wanted to shake him and force him to tell her everything, but that wasn't fair. That would make her like Verity. "I still don't understand why Verity would let Monica back into her life. As kids we vowed we'd never have anything to do with her again."

Gabe blew out a breath. "Monica couldn't get her dream job acting, so she became an influencer selling make-up and jewellery instead. She was losing subscribers and was convinced it was because she looked too old, so she convinced Verity to help her.

She passed Verity off as her sister, can you believe? That's where the name Langley-Moore came in. Monica told her she needed to change her name to fit in with the brand. I tried to convince Verity it was crazy, but Monica was showering her with jewellery and beautiful clothes and Verity couldn't resist."

Clever woman. Verity had loved jewellery for as long as Ella could remember. As a little girl she'd dressed up in pretty dresses, cheap beads, fake pearls and tiaras, then she'd spin around, asking Ella if she looked like a princess.

"Verity said she wouldn't go unless I came too," Gabe said. "That's why Monica paid for my studies and arranged with her partner to get me a job in his real-estate firm."

"I doubt that was the only reason. You've always been smart. You're obviously an asset to their business. After all, they made you a partner."

He looked away. "Being made partner trapped me there. Even when Verity and I didn't marry."

"But why did Verity say you were married if you weren't?"

Gabe sighed. "Ella, so much has happened. So much that's hard to explain."

"You can at least try."

He blinked hard and a band tightened around her chest. This man who had once been her closest friend was hurting and she wasn't helping.

"I didn't want to disappoint my parents." He rubbed the back of his neck. "I didn't want them to know I was living with Verity outside of marriage." He studied his shoes and she did, too. Expensive-looking shoes. A rich man's shoes. She didn't know this man.

"I wasn't living for God and I made a complete mess of it," he said. "But I'm different now."

"You believe in God now?"

"With all my heart." The passion in his voice surprised her. "I'm still learning, but God has changed me. I'm not the man I once was. Of course, having Lacy has helped with that, too."

She could see that, but she missed the old Gabe. She resented the years that had passed, the circumstances she was helpless to change.

"I suppose you plan to take Lacy back to America when this is all over." Her voice was filled with a coldness she despised yet couldn't seem to control. Lacy was Gabe's daughter, and he was hurting, too.

"Not necessarily."

That was a surprise.

He turned so he could look directly at her and the light from the sun reflected in his eyes. They glistened with unshed tears. "El, I'm angry, too. You're not the only one struggling here."

El. That was Verity's name for her. Gabe had never called her that before. Only Ella or Gabriella when he felt like it. The way he said the name softened her and reached the emotions she was trying to hide. She swallowed against the lump in her throat as he continued speaking.

"I don't want to go back to the States. I know I owe my financial security to the place, and I know I even have a bit of an accent now, but I hate how much of my life I allowed to be stolen from me. I hate that Verity and I went so far away from you and your family."

"So why did you?"

He flinched. "I thought I loved her."

"You say 'thought' and yet you were engaged. If things really got too difficult, why were you still engaged?"

"We had our rough patches, secrets some people would never guess, and there were times I wanted to leave, but I prayed a lot about it, and I knew that God wanted me to stay. And I learned to love her with love that was a choice, not an infatuation or a changing emotion. True love. The kind that God gives."

Wow, he really did take faith seriously now. But did he really love Verity, or did he think he should commit to her because they had a daughter? And was he saying Verity had been an infatuation? Running her finger along the wood grain pattern of the verandah didn't help calm the storm of emotions inside.

"She had so much ambition, so much potential." Gabe appeared to now be talking to himself as much as he was to her.

"Yeah, but she gave it all up for you, Gabe." Ella's voice broke. "She loved you more than anything else."

To her dismay, his chin trembled. "No," he said shaking his head. "No, Ella."

Was he denying that Verity loved him, or was he trying to deny the fact that she was gone, fighting against the reality they now had to live in? He looked so lost, so broken that the same protective instinct she'd felt toward Lacy rose up within. Unable to help herself, she slid across and put an arm around his broad shoulders in a side hug. He turned and returned the hug. She buried her head in his neck, knowing that despite the unfamiliar smell of his expensive cologne, the harsh feel of his pressed suit, that the Gabe she'd met all those years ago was still in there somewhere.

Strange how she felt closer to Gabe Vance in that moment than she ever had to her departed sister. She and Verity had never shared such grief, such understanding. And Verity was the cause of this deep, unbreakable connection she now shared with Gabe.

Gabe sighed a deep, shuddery sigh then pulled away from her and stood. He reached a hand down to Ella and she allowed him to pull her up beside him.

"Ella, there's something important I need to talk to you about."

Chapter Eighteen

Ella half expected an apology or explanation for Verity's death and so his next words left her reeling.

"Lacy needs family. Real family." He couldn't seem to meet her eyes. "I'm helping the police with their investigation, so I will be coming and going until this is all sorted, but after that, I will have to go back to the States. And I think it's best if I don't take Lacy with me."

"What?" Any connection she'd just felt with him was severed. How could he? "She's just lost her mother and you plan to leave her in another country without her father?"

And you plan to leave me here to grieve alone?

Gabe swallowed hard. "Ella, we think Monica wants to take Lacy. She claims I'm not Lacy's real father."

Would the shocks ever stop coming?

"So get a DNA test. Prove that you are." A thought stopped her cold. "Unless ... you think you aren't?"

"I'm not bowing to that woman's demands." Gabe's expression turned dark. "I *am* Lacy's father and I want her here, safe, as far away from that woman as she can be. I want you to be Lacy's guardian."

Ella tried to speak. Cleared her throat, gave up.

"She needs you," Gabe said.

"Gabe, no. I don't understand. Why would you give up your daughter just because someone makes up some crazy rumour? Where's your fight?"

Gabe rubbed his hands over his eyes. "Maybe I'm tired of fighting."

"You wouldn't fight for your own daughter? I know how it feels to be abandoned, Gabe. Don't do it, please. For Lacy's sake."

"It's the last thing I want to do. It will break my heart, but I'm trying to do what's best for my little girl. I honestly believe it's what God wants me to do." Gabe's voice was heavy with sadness. "I need to protect her from Monica. She tried to convince Verity to take my name off Lacy's birth certificate. She offered Verity a lot of money if she'd do it, but she said no."

"But why would Monica do that?"

"I think she wants to claim Lacy as her own child. She's all about appearance and she has an obsession about staying young. I think she's mentally unstable, to be honest. She didn't want Verity all those years ago because having a child made her feel old and held her back. But she told Verity that if she had a child now, it would make her appear younger to her viewers and she could keep up her youthful image. She believes it would be to her advantage." Anger darkened Gabe's eyes. "She believes the world revolves around her."

Like Verity had.

Ella's mind raced. Would Verity have put Gabe's name on Lacy's birth certificate if he wasn't her real father? And why was Verity murdered?

So many questions. She didn't want to voice the one that kept swirling around her head, but she needed to. "Gabe, do... do you think Monica has something to do with Verity's murder?"

His gaze held hers. "I do."

"She'd murder her own daughter so she could take her child?"

"Or get someone else to. Monica is cold, El. There's something evil about her."

"So why would she try to murder me too?"

"If she thinks you might get in the way of her claiming Lacy, she'd do it."

"Do they have any proof?"

He winced. "I can't tell you anything else. You'll need to ask Tait. But El, I told the police I'd like you to have Lacy with you in the cottage. See if you feel you can care for her, love her. Maybe even adopt her one day. She's so like you. Sometimes when I look at her, when she gives me that shy smile, I feel like I've been given a second chance, to make up for what I did to you."

Her heart thudded. What did he think he'd done to her?

She swallowed the lump in her throat. Of course she wouldn't say no to taking Lacy, but deep within was a fear she was being manipulated, something she'd vowed never to let happen again.

"I do have a life of my own, Gabe," she said. "I've got a job. A good job."

"But what about your dreams?"

She made a scoffing sound. "My dreams? What do you know about my dreams?"

"Your ... your dreams of a family."

Seriously? Indignation rose. "You think I'm still stuck in my teenage fantasies? You think what you and Verity had makes me think dreams ever come true? I was a child and thought the world could be beautiful and pain free. I thought Cinderella stories were possible."

"Ella, I'm not manipulating you. I promise." His hand came to rest on her shoulder, unsettling her and warming her all at once. How did he read her so well? "I just want what's best for Lacy. And I think it would be good for you, too. Children are so innocent and free. I saw the way you softened the moment Lacy was in your arms. Having a child like her brings down protective walls, fear of love—"

"Oh, Gabe Vance." He was way too close to the truth. "Grow a beard!"

Her words came out on impulse, out of habit. She cringed. How embarrassing.

He snorted softly. "I grew a beard just so you could never say that again." A hoarse chuckle escaped him. "But you're never going to let me grow up, are you?"

She eyed his suit, his tie, his beard, met his gaze. The truth was, she'd do anything to bring back the immature, boyish friend she'd met as a fifteen-year-old. If only he'd never walked into her lounge room and spotted Verity. Maybe Verity would still be here now.

But Lacy would not. The thought stirred her. She felt so deeply for the little girl she'd only just met, but what was she supposed to do with these conflicting emotions? Except be there for her. The truth was, Lacy did need her. And she needed Lacy, too.

"El," Gabe said, "I just wish you would allow yourself to be the loving, affectionate person you are deep down inside." His voice was low, intense, unsettling. "You won't let yourself dream any more in case those dreams are crushed."

Ella shook her head. The day had been overwhelming and this conversation was too much. It was all too much. "Gabe, can we leave it for now? I'm so tired. Can we talk tomorrow?"

Gabe nodded. "Mum will have Lacy tonight so you can have a good sleep. But please, please consider doing this for Lacy."

She couldn't deny him when he begged her like that. Not that she'd ever planned on denying him. It would be her honour to love Lacy and protect her. To tell her about her mother and make sure she knew she was loved. But the disbelief and dismay that Gabe would so easily abandon his child went soul-crushingly deep.

***

All night, a little girl dressed in pink filled Ella's mind and dreams. A little girl with eyes like hers and a mother named Verity.

As the sun rose, she searched through the bag that had been packed for her, putting aside work clothes and pulling on a pair of jeans and t-shirt, grateful they'd found some of the few casual clothes she owned.

She walked out into the cool morning air, to the big house where Lacy was sleeping. All looked peaceful. Savage nodded to her from where he stood near the fence line. She lifted her hand in a wave, then sat on the edge of the verandah, drawing in deep breaths. She ran her hands down her jeans.

A door opened and Margo stepped out, Lacy in her arms.

"Couldn't sleep either?" she asked.

Ella shook her head as she stood to greet them.

Lacy wriggled to get down and scampered over to Ella. Swallowing a lump in her throat, Ella welcomed Lacy into her arms. Lacy snuggled in, resting her head on Ella's shoulder. Then she closed her eyes.

Margo's eyes met Ella's. "She needs you."

Ella looked away. Gabe no doubt told his mother he'd asked her to be Lacy's guardian.

Margo seemed to read her thoughts.

"Ella, I know Gabe seems—what's the word?—rather pushy right now, but he feels like he's drowning and he's struggling for breath. He's used to ordering people around; it's his job. And whenever he feels lost he automatically goes into that mode. Please don't let his manner affect your decision. Think of Lacy."

Ella managed a smile. Gabe hadn't been pushy really. Desperate, might be a better word.

"It's okay, Mrs. Vance—"

"Margo."

"Margo. Now that I've met Lacy, I don't think I'd want to leave her. Ever." She rubbed the little girl's back.

Margo took a deep breath that sounded something like relief, then reached over and swept a strand of Lacy's hair back off her forehead. Then she wrapped both of them in a hug.

Ella tried to control the emotions that welled up. Margo Vance was a good mother. Memories resurfaced. The way she had envied Gabe his mother, so poised and beautiful, with a soft, compassionate heart. Margo had understood her disappointment the day she'd tripped at the athletics carnival, and she understood her grief today. What gave a woman such perception and compassion?

Why hadn't this woman been asked to look after little Lacy? She would be the best person to do it if Gabe wasn't going to look after his little girl. She was missing something here.

"Good morning."

They all looked up at the sound of Gabe's deep voice and Lacy struggled in Ella's arms.

"Daddy!" She ran to him. He lifted her, but his eyes didn't light up at the sight of her like they did yesterday. Ella wondered at his lack of response. How could he not show warmth to his daughter? One look at his face gave her the answer. There were dark rings beneath his eyes and there was a shadow of heavy sadness about him. Ella doubted he had slept at all last night.

But why did he still wear a suit? He clearly wouldn't be working today. Was he trying to prove something? Making sure he was far removed from the impish schoolboy she had once lo—liked so much? His beard was enough to give him an air of authority if he wanted it. He reminded Ella of Mr. Dale, their economics teacher back in high school.

"Play hide-a-boo?" Lacy asked, bouncing in his arms. When he didn't answer immediately, she reached up and mussed his hair.

His hand caught hers. "Not now, sweetie. Later?"

"Yay!" Lacy giggled as Gabe set her back down. She then toddled along the verandah, running her hands along the potted flowers. "So pwitty. So pwitty."

Ella couldn't help smiling. "What's hide-a-boo?"

"You tell me." One corner of Gabe's mouth lifted. "I've come to think it's whatever Lacy wants it to be on any given day. And the rules might change in the middle of the game."

Ella's smile widened. "Well, I guess she'll teach me then." Could the child be any more adorable?

"So you'll take her? Give this a chance?"

Ella glanced into Margo's eyes and saw the message there. *Don't be annoyed at his assumption. Gabe is trying to stay afloat. That's why he's acting this way.*

And she understood. Wasn't that why she'd acted so cold toward him at times? Why she'd frozen when he'd kissed her all those years ago? She'd been lost and overwhelmed.

It was obvious he was used to people doing what he wanted. He gazed steadily at her, expecting her to resign from her job and care for his little girl because he wanted her to.

How dare you assume I'll take her? That you know me so well? I'm not Verity. We are very different.

Had been so very different.

Her heart ached as she watched Lacy reach for a butterfly and giggle as it flew away. Of course Gabe had known she'd care for her. Love her. Who wouldn't?

"I'd need to move once we're out of protective custody or whatever you call this," she said. "I only have a one-bedroom apartment in Sydney."

Gabe didn't blink. "I have a place in the US I could recommend. I'll buy it for you. It's in a beautiful little town called Trinity Lakes, across the other side of the country from Monica, and I've got some friends at the Bible college there who would look after you."

Ella bristled. "You expect me to resign from work and move to the US? Are you serious?"

"You won't need to work. I have the money, Ella. And if you take this place I have in mind, Lacy won't need to grow up in the city."

"So you assume I don't want to work, or don't you think working mothers exist?"

A muscle jumped in his jaw. "I just ... it would mean I could see Lacy more often, and Mum's agreed to move there too, if you and Lacy do. If you want to work, she could look after Lacy during the day."

"Oh." Ella glanced at Margo. The woman's eyes were filled with hope. She wanted her nearby. Or Lacy, anyway. "I'll think about it."

If Lacy couldn't have her mother and father around, it would be good for her to at least have her grandmother nearby. Especially a loving one like Margo. Ella knew what it was like to grow up without a mother figure, and she didn't want that for Lacy.

"Great." Gabe gave a satisfied nod. "I'll talk to the realtor and negotiate a price."

Seriously? *Don't push me*, Ella wanted to snap, but instead she glared at him, trying to swallow back her anger. Here he was, taking over her whole life. Is this what he'd done to Verity? No, she couldn't imagine Verity letting anyone push her to do anything she didn't want to do.

She forced herself to breathe out her frustration. "Give me a chance to decide if I want to work, first. To decide if I even want the place you're looking at."

"Don't rush her, Gabe." Margo touched his arm. "There's a lot going on and we all need time to adjust. Give her a chance to decide for herself."

Rather than feel grateful for her support, Ella looked at Gabe's mother suspiciously. Did Margo want to hold things off because she wanted to care for the little girl herself? No one could truly be as selfless as she seemed to be. Surely she couldn't truly be happy about Gabe asking Ella to care for Lacy, the girl she was a grandmother to?

"I don't need help," Ella said, looking pointedly at Gabe. "Yours or anyone else's. I can look after myself."

Gabe's eyes widened, then his mouth twitched like he might be amused. "We all need a bit of help every now and then, El." He nodded toward Savage, who stood just out of hearing distance, his stance and expression alert.

He was right of course. She needed help and protection right now. They all did. But he didn't have to be so smug about being right. And how would he feel if he was grumpy and she found it funny? Not that she'd ever seen him grumpy. Not really. Sad and sorrowful, yes. A little bossy right now. But grumpy? No.

She tried to hold back her annoyance as she stared him down. "I might be in protective custody for now, but I'm a capable adult and I still have a mind of my own."

Gabe rubbed his beard. "I've never doubted it. I'll wait to hear what you decide."

"Okay." Her shoulders relaxed, but she still felt like he was humouring her. She had no idea what to make of him. Gabe Vance as a man was a stranger to her.

***

Ella was surprised to find Tait Ellison at her door later that evening. She let him inside and invited him into the lounge room.

"I've been assigned your case," he said as he sat down. "I get to keep an eye on you and Lacy," his look turned apologetic, "and annoy you with questions at the same time."

"Interrogate me?" She was only half joking.

"Sort of."

She sat down and pulled a cushion onto her lap. "That's okay." At least it meant she could see his familiar face.

Tait leaned forward, his eyes softening. "Ella, I'm sorry you're going through this."

"Yeah. I know you understand, having been through it yourself." She picked at a thread on the cushion.

"Well, to some extent, but what happened to me was my own fault."

"No, Tait," she said, hating that he'd blame himself. "I'm sure that's not true."

"It is the truth, Ella." He gave a self-deprecating smile. "I could blame it on bad parents, a rough childhood, a criminal brother, but all the choices I made were my own. It's okay though. Even when I was still a criminal, God proved to me that He's real and showed me He loves me. All I had to do was ask His forgiveness and He totally turned my life around."

She frowned. "You were still a criminal when you became a Christian?"

"Yeah." He rubbed the back of his neck. "I was actually in the process of trying to steal the identity of a man who'd been killed in a train accident."

"Excuse me?"

He grimaced. "I know, hero to humanity right here. It was so my brother Joel could take on his identity when I helped break him out of prison. The dead man's name was Toby Cardelle and I went to his home town of Barrawi and convinced his family I was Toby's friend. The more I found out about Toby, the easier it would be to steal his identity. I soon discovered the Cardelles were Christians and I witnessed their love of God and people. It shone from them, and even though they were grieving the loss of Toby, they had this peace about them."

Peace? How could anyone have peace in the midst of grief? She hugged the cushion against her chest.

"And then," he continued, "their daughter, who had lost her vision, was miraculously healed. You can't deny God's existence when you witness something like that. That was when I realised I was on the wrong side and was going the wrong way. But then God turned my life around, let me know He made me for a purpose, to do good, to shine light in this dark world, to not give in and surrender to the darkness."

Surrender to the darkness. Ella pictured the stars shining in the night sky. They didn't surrender. They shone in the darkness, giving hope and light to all who looked up to see them.

"I wish God would do the same for me," she whispered.

Tait's intense gaze captured hers. "He will. He is. Just look for Him, Ella. Look for His hand, for His light. Let Him turn your world around."

She couldn't respond for the lump in her throat. Was God in all of this? How could He be? How in the world could He turn something as awful as death into life and hope and light?

"I'm praying for you," Tait said. "That you will see God, and that you will know He sees *you*."

She blinked hard. It felt like God really did care, that He was looking after her, letting her know He saw her, that He hadn't overlooked her. God had known she needed a friend, someone whose words offered hope. A friend like Tait.

Chapter Nineteen

Ella looked around at the items that had been delivered to her door. Furniture, boxes, clothes. Everything from her flat, they'd said. She could decorate the cottage with her own things. Make it home. Lacy's things would be brought over from the main house later in the afternoon.

"Does this mean I'll be here a long time?" Ella had asked Tait.

"Not if I can help it, but you know these things. They take time."

Ella had wanted to demand dates, demand more information, but she had to accept everything was unknown. She had no control over any of this.

She hadn't asked Gabe how much support he planned to give her for looking after Lacy, but she knew it would be more than sufficient. Swallowing back pride she hadn't known she had, she shook her head at the irony of it all. Gabe Vance, the boy from the newspaper, was supporting her after all. Not in the home of her dreams and not as her husband, but supporting her just the same.

"It's me who's making the sacrifice," she reassured herself. "Taking on a child that isn't mine."

She glanced once more around the room. It all felt so strange, and she felt numb. But she had a job to do, and that would keep her going. If she had anything to do with it, Lacy would never want for anything, especially love and attention.

She jumped as a knock came at the door.

"Ella, it's me." Gabe. She opened the door to let him in. He stepped inside and looked around at all the boxes. "I came to see if you need any help."

What made him think she needed his help with everything? She glared a challenge at him. "I'm sure I can manage, thank you."

He winced and turned to leave.

Guilt niggled. She didn't need to snap at him. "Gabe," she called after him more gently, "I'm okay. Really."

He came to stand directly before her, looking uncertain. He rubbed a hand down his dark beard. "You're not okay, Ella. And I'm not either. We'll probably never be okay again. But can't we at least support each other instead of, instead of…"

Was he trying to say she was being unreasonable? "What? Instead of what?"

"Instead of this." He waved his hand helplessly. "This is exactly what I'm talking about. You're so angry with me and I can't handle it right now. I don't have the energy to deal with it."

He looked so tired and defeated that Ella looked away. She knew she was being unreasonable and adding to his pain, and she didn't know why. Nothing made sense right now.

"I'm sorry," she whispered. "I'll try."

"Thanks." His voice came out raspy and she wanted to cry, but held it in.

Gabe turned to leave and she put out a hand to stop him. "Some of these boxes are heavy," she admitted. "I want to pile them over in that corner and then sort them. You … you could help with that. If you want."

He nodded and began shuffling them toward the corner, his movements stilted. That suit must be so hot and uncomfortable.

"Don't you own anything other than suits?"

He looked back at her. "I have some jeans somewhere. Back home."

In America.

A reminder that he was only here for a short time and then he'd return to the US. With or without her and Lacy.

She worked silently by his side until the boxes were moved.

"What about the furniture?" he asked.

"I don't know where I want it yet. Tait said he and Savage can help later." And she needed space. Space to think and sort out all these overwhelming feelings.

Gabe nodded, then turned with a wave and left before Ella had a chance to thank him. But at least she now had privacy as she got the feel of her new temporary home.

In silence she studied the room that was to be Lacy's. The tiny little bed made her smile. Then she saw a soft toy rabbit even more ragged than the pink teddy Lacy now clung to at all times.

The toy rabbit had been Verity's. Unwanted tears stung her eyes. Verity had clung to that rabbit when her mother first left. Ella had tried to comfort her, but she'd huddled in the corner of the room, tears streaming down her angelic little face, that rabbit tucked securely under her arm.

It didn't seem fair that Verity's little girl had to go through the same thing.

***

Gabe brought Lacy to the cottage that evening, holding her close against his chest.

"Mommy?" Lacy said, her gaze searching the room. Ella wanted to cry at the hope in the little girl's expression.

Gabe pushed a strand of wispy hair from his daughter's face. "Lace, remember I said Aunty Ella is going to look after you?"

The brightness in Lacy's eyes faded into confusion as she looked up at Ella.

Gabe lowered her to the floor before squatting down and looking directly into her eyes. "Aunty Ella is Mummy's sister. You can call her Ella."

"Mommy El," Lacy said, her American accent coming through again.

Ella looked questioningly to Gabe. Did it bother him that Lacy insisted on calling her Mommy? She couldn't read his closed expression. Her heart ached to see him tease and laugh freely again.

"Mum set up her room earlier and will bring some other things over later."

Gabe's abrupt change of subject showed he wasn't ready to deal with the issue of what Lacy called her. Or else he didn't want to traumatise the girl any more than she already had been. "I saw."

"Mum made sure she has everything she needs."

Ella nodded again, wanting to ask why he hadn't been the one to do that. He was obviously a good father, but had Verity been the one who cared for all Lacy's day to day needs? Had Gabe been too busy with work? Had he lived with Verity and Lacy? They were engaged, after all. So many questions she didn't yet feel free to ask.

"We'll be fine." Ella dismissed him with a wave of her hand.

He cast her an uncertain look before bending down to take Lacy in his arms again. "I love you, Lacy."

Her chest thudded. Love. Was it love that made Gabe willing to leave Lacy behind now that Verity was gone? What if the truth was he no longer considered Lacy to be his concern?

They waved goodbye to Gabe and then Lacy stared up at Ella, eyes wide with questions.

Ella forced a bright smile. "So, Lacy, what's for tea?"

She smiled and pointed to the kitchen pantry. Did she know what was in there? Ella had no idea what a two-year-old would eat and so she opened the doors and let her choose for herself.

Rice Bubbles was her definite preference so Ella poured her a bowl. She added milk and handed Lacy a spoon, but the little girl quickly became frustrated and used her hands instead.

Ella couldn't help laughing. Lacy sat with hands full of Rice Bubbles, trying to shove them in her mouth. Instead, they stuck to her hands and chin and nose.

How had Verity handled the grottiness of a child? She had always liked things spotless. Well, Ella was different. She could handle it. In fact, she sat down beside Lacy, poured a bowl of Rice Bubbles and began to eat them the same way.

Lacy giggled, smiling impishly at Ella. And in that giggle Ella caught a glimpse of her childhood friend, Gabe.

"I love you, Lacy Vance," Ella said softly and was startled by the way the little girl jumped down from her chair and flew into her arms. Rice Bubbles transferred from her hands and face onto Ella's, but all she was aware of was the warmth of the little body clinging to her as though holding on for dear life.

"We're going to be okay, Lacy," Ella whispered, tears clogging her throat. "It's all going to be okay."

She hoped with all her heart she could keep that promise.

Chapter Twenty

Ella awoke with a start to blood-curdling screams. Her heart pounded in her chest as the awful sound assaulted her ears. It took a moment to realise where she was and who was screaming.

"Lacy!" She flung off her blankets and ran into Lacy's bedroom. The two-year-old was on the floor, thrashing like a wild animal. Her eyes were wide open as she flung herself around and screamed until she was hoarse. Her hair and clothes were dishevelled and fear rose up within Ella. If Lacy kept on like this she was sure to bash herself against something and get seriously hurt.

"Hey, Lacy, it's okay." She raised her voice to catch her attention above the screams. When that didn't work she rushed to her, arms open, only to find herself struck and shoved out of the way. She tried again to hold her, only to have Lacy lash out, her tiny elbow coming in contact with Ella's lip. She tasted blood, felt it trickle down her chin.

Panic rose like a flood inside her, threatening to drown any reasonable thoughts. She was completely alone and helpless with full responsibility for this child. She had no idea how to deal with this. Lacy had appeared so weary and calm before bed and had settled easily. Now this.

Lacy let out another scream and Ella ran for her phone. She called Margo Vance's number.

"Margo speaking," her voice, rusty from sleep, came over the phone.

"It's me, Ella," Ella shouted above Lacy's screams.

"And that's Lacy," Margo finished for her. "I'm on my way."

Ella paced as she waited for Margo to arrive. How could a child scream and thrash for so long? Where did all that energy come from? Why would nothing console her? It was as though she couldn't see or hear Ella, still in a world of sleep, though she was wide awake.

Margo rushed in, and had she not been so tense, Ella would have struggled not to laugh. The beautiful, poised woman had hair poking up in all directions and was wearing the kind of nightdress Ella would expect to see on a teenager. Thin and short with the words, "Wake up and smell the coffee" splashed down the front. It was clear she had rushed straight out the door with no thought for her appearance.

Ella followed her into Lacy's room where the little girl was still thrashing, though little sound was coming from her now-hoarse throat. To Ella's surprise, Margo just stood there, watching. Then she turned to Ella.

"Night terrors," she said.

"Night terrors?"

"Yes. Gabe's older sister Naomi had them at the same age. We'd just moved from Cessnock to Albury. She was about Lacy's age. It was too much for her little mind to comprehend."

"So what do we do?"

"Nothing."

"Nothing?" What kind of hard-hearted person could watch a child suffer like that and do nothing to try to comfort her?

"That's right. Waking her, if it's possible, will just confuse and frighten her even more. Holding her will probably make her panic or injure herself."

"Or me." Ella indicated the blood on her lip with a wry smile.

Margo looked sympathetic and reached for a tissue from the box on Lacy's bedside table. Ella dabbed at the blood. Thankfully the bleeding had settled.

"I know it's awful to watch, but it will pass," Margo assured her. "And Lacy will probably have no idea about it in the morning."

As though on cue, Lacy suddenly slumped and lay still, calm in peaceful sleep. Ella could hardly believe it after what she had witnessed only minutes earlier. Margo gently lifted her back into her bed where the little girl still didn't stir. Ella watched as Margo pushed a strand of hair back from Lacy's hot, sweat-drenched brow and sat on the bed just gazing at her granddaughter.

Emotion rose within her, coupled with relief and exhaustion. "I don't think I can do this," she whispered, holding back a sob. "Margo, I feel so helpless. I have no idea about children. You should be the one looking after her."

Margo turned and her expression was gentle. "No, Ella, you'll do fine. Do you think Verity knew what to do? Motherhood is a steep learning curve and new experiences will arise all the time. Both you and Lacy will be enriched through it all. Me? I've had my time of raising children. I loved it, but I don't have the strength to do it again. I'm getting older and I'm not as strong and healthy as I used to be. I'm fit to be a grandmother now, and a grandmother's job is to help the mother love and learn and grow. I want to do that for you."

Ella felt her chin quiver and bit her lip as she studied Margo Vance. How could a woman in a nightdress with messy hair still emanate poise and beauty in such a striking way?

"Thank you," was all she could manage.

Margo seemed to understand. "We both need our sleep." She rose to leave. "I'll come over first thing in the morning."

"For breakfast?"

She smiled. "If that's what you'd like."

"It is. I have no idea what to feed a two-year-old, and Rice Bubbles probably isn't a good idea for every meal."

Margo let out a hearty laugh. She gave Ella a quick hug and was gone.

Ella sighed as she went back to bed. Why couldn't her step-mother have been like Margo? A woman who put the needs of others first and cared more for them than for her own image. Margo in a nightdress was far more beautiful than a woman like Monica in an evening gown.

In that moment Ella knew she wanted to be like Margo. To have whatever it was that made the woman who she was.

Chapter Twenty-One

Margo was right. Lacy remembered nothing of her night terrors and seemed quite settled when she ran into Ella's room the following morning. Her hair was tousled from sleep, and her teddy bear was tucked securely under one arm. She climbed up into the bed beside Ella with a shy smile and snuggled in. Ella smiled back as she hugged the toddler.

She managed to dress Lacy and bring her into the kitchen just as Margo knocked on the door.

Lacy's eyes lit up and she ran to the door. "Daddy?"

"No, sweetie. It's Grandma." Ella unlocked the door. Should she tell the little girl her daddy had gone away for a while? Or was that what she'd been told about her mother? She didn't want to scare the child.

"Good morning," Margo met them with a huge smile and hug for both of them. She held up a bag. "I brought some eggs from the chook pen out the back of the big house. I thought I could make scrambled eggs on toast."

Ella beamed. "Sounds great. Thank you."

Lacy ran into the living room to play with a little toy house that looked new. No doubt it was. Ella leaned in close and spoke quietly to Margo.

"Is there some kind of book I can read about bringing up little girls who've lost their mothers? I'm totally lost here."

Margo cracked another egg into the bowl, then turned to look at Ella.

"There's nothing like experience," she said. "You were a little girl who lost her mother, weren't you?"

Ella nodded.

"Do you remember much of your childhood? Of the feelings, the needs?"

"Too much."

Margo shook her head. "No, not too much. What if God allowed you to remember it so you can help Lacy? I believe you are the perfect person to help Lacy. Empathy and love are powerful and healing."

"You sound like you speak from experience."

Margo smiled. "I do. And do you know who healed me the most? Who showed me the greatest empathy, understanding, and love?"

Ella shook her head.

"God. Through Jesus. My childhood wasn't easy, Ella. I lost my father and younger brother in a car accident when I was only seven. My mother was never the same after that. There was so much fear, confusion and pain. Mum struggled emotionally and could never stick at a job. Sometimes we would go without food. But I always sensed there was Someone looking out for me. And I found out who He is one day speaking to a lady in the local church op-shop. I was twelve and I'd gone in to buy some clothes. The lady cared for my physical needs, gave me clothes and food as well, but there was just something about her. She shared the love of Jesus with me, told me Jesus loved me, urged me to talk to Him, to get to know

Him." Margo's eyes shone. "I knew she spoke the truth and that day I came to believe. She picked me up for church each Sunday and as I learned more about God and His love, He transformed me, healed me, made me new from the inside out. Now I know I'm never alone."

Ella bit her lip. Should she tell Margo about the Someone who spoke to her when she was a little girl? Who wrapped her in warmth and love as she looked out at the stars?

"Ell-ell?"

Ella smiled at Lacy's attempt to say her name. She toddled into the room, reaching out her hand and beckoning.

"You want me to come?"

Lacy nodded, grabbing Ella's pinkie finger and leading her into the living room. There she'd tipped a moving box on its side.

"House," she said and climbed in, pulling the flaps down and closing herself in. Then she pushed one out and peeked out, a smile lighting her face. "Boo!"

Ella laughed. "Is that your window?"

Lacy nodded and closed herself in again. Then she knocked on the box and made a ringing noise.

Ella peeked in. "Are you at the door?"

Lacy threw open the flap of the lid and beamed. "Come in."

"Um ..." Ella chuckled. "I don't think I can fit in there, Lacy. We'd need a much bigger box."

Lacy seemed to understand. She crawled out of her box and pointed to a larger box in the corner containing Ella's linen.

"In," she said with a beseeching expression. "Ell-ell in."

"Sorry Lacy, I'm too big. Even for that one. I might get stuck in there."

"Breakfast is ready," Margo called, and Ella watched, relieved as Lacy flew into the kitchen.

Margo's eyes twinkled at Ella over Lacy's head. "Toddlers are hard work," she mouthed.

That was for sure. How was she going to keep this little livewire entertained on her own? She was so grateful for Margo right now.

"Why don't you take Lacy out for a bit?" Margo suggested after breakfast as Ella cleaned Lacy's face and hands. "Go shopping, maybe?"

Lacy's eyes widened. "Shops? Toy?"

"Are we allowed to go shopping?" Ella didn't want to disappoint Lacy, but she wasn't sure what the rules were. "I don't even have a card anymore."

"Oh." Margo bit her lip. "I just assumed. Hang on." She picked up her phone and pressed the screen. "Tait, is Ella allowed to take Lacy shopping?"

Ella listened to lots of 'mm-hm's' before Margo ended the call and smiled at her. "Tait's on his way with a card for you. He'll come along but stay in the background. It's a small-town shopping centre and should be pretty safe. I'll head back home if you don't mind."

"But—"

"You'll be fine, Ella. Trust your instincts. Trust God. And Tait."

"Toy?" Lacy asked again, appearing to follow every word.

"Sure." Ella smiled. "We can buy a toy."

Lacy bounced in excitement and raced for her shoes by the front door as Margo headed back to the house.

Ella helped Lacy with her shoes, fascinated by her perfectly shaped little feet and toes. With a pang she remembered helping five-year-old Verity lace up her shoes. They were in the days when

Verity still relied on her and looked up to her. When the competition hadn't yet begun.

Ella swallowed hard, noticing the concern in Lacy's expression as she studied her face. "Sad?" she asked.

Ella stroked her soft hair. "I'm okay." She needed to hide her feelings better. "Let's go," she said with forced brightness, reaching for her hand.

"No." Lacy snatched it away. "Mommy hold. Not you."

Who? Margo? Or Verity? The little girl's rejection stung, but Ella understood. Lacy hardly knew her.

"Um, Mummy's not here," she murmured.

Lacy frowned. "Yes, look!" She held out her hand as though it was being held by her mother. She then held out her other hand to Ella.

Hesitantly, Ella took it, relieved when Lacy grasped it tight. Was it healthy for Lacy to imagine Verity was there? She'd ask Margo later. Together, she and Lacy walked out to where Tait now sat with the car running outside their door. She was glad Margo seemed confident in her ability to be a mother, because she felt completely inadequate.

***

Ella wheeled the shopping trolley through the aisles, exulting in the freedom to do something so normal. Tait had given her a non-personalised card to use for payment and sent her into the shop with Lacy while he waited at the car. Lacy hadn't taken long to choose what she wanted – a colouring in book, some pencils and a soft, fluffy toy cow. Ella added a packet of Tim-Tams to the trolley. Well, she and Lacy deserved some treats after all they'd been through.

"Wow," Lacy exclaimed at the top of her voice. "Lots of stuff." She caught the eye of an elderly couple shopping nearby. "Lots of stuff," she repeated.

Ella's face grew warm. Take back that thought about this shopping trip being normal. Trying to cover her embarrassment, she put another packet of Tim-Tams in the trolley without thought.

"Two?" Lacy questioned at the top of her voice.

Well, look who'd found her voice. "Um … um, I thought you might like them," Ella muttered.

"Yes," Lacy agreed. "And Arlo."

Arlo? Who was Arlo? Ella's stomach dropped in confusion, and at the same time, Lacy panicked.

"Mommy! Where's Mommy?" She held up the hand she had reserved for her mother to hold.

People were now staring and Ella searched her mind for how to respond. So much for keeping a low profile.

"Right here, remember," she improvised, pointing. "She's holding your hand."

Yes, she appeared strange, but it worked. Lacy let out a sigh of relief as she smiled and people turned away either no longer interested or smothering smiles. Ella wasn't amused. She would prefer climbing in and out of boxes any day to going through this. She went directly to the check-out as fast as she could and piled their items on the counter.

Suddenly Lacy ducked underneath the counter. "Scared," she said, shaking. "Monster."

"A monster?" Ella looked around, while the check-out girl waited for her to put the next item from the trolley up on the counter. "Where?"

Lacy pointed up to where the check-out girl stood.

Unable to help herself, Ella let out a burst of laughter. The poor check-out girl looked bemused.

"Sorry, she has a good imagination," Ella said.

The check-out girl suddenly grinned. "My brother would say it's not too much of a stretch to think I'm a monster. So I might keep this to myself."

Relieved, Ella grinned back. "I don't think I'll be telling many people about this, either."

Ella paid while Lacy tugged at her jeans.

"Go," she urged, still pretending to shake and shooting wide-eyed looks at the 'monster' who was now handing Ella her receipt. Ella had never seen a monster with such bleached blonde hair and bright blue eyes.

"Okay, let's go," Ella agreed and smiled gratefully at the check-out girl. "Thanks." She tried to rush Lacy through the door and out to the car.

But Lacy pulled back. "Wait. Arlo stuck."

Arlo again? "Stuck?" Ella pulled back on the trolley looking around for Tait. She could do with his help right now. And who was Arlo?

"Stuck." Lacy pointed to the now closed automatic doors.

And so Ella waited patiently for the doors to open again so 'Arlo' could free himself and come with them to the car.

Tait came to meet them and took the trolley so Ella could hold Lacy's hand to cross the car park. "How was it?"

Ella let out a big sigh. "I don't know that Lacy understands what it means to keep a low profile."

"You do look a bit frazzled."

"Frazzled doesn't begin to describe it."

Tait loaded the shopping in the car while Ella put Lacy in her car seat. She tightened the straps, then opened the front passenger door ready to sit and rest.

"No. Mommy sit," Lacy said, pointing to the front seat.

Ella should have known it wouldn't be straightforward. "How about Mummy sits next to you?"

Lacy shook her head and pointed to the seat beside her. "Arlo and Ell-ell."

Tait grinned at her as he came to the driver's side. "Better sit in the back so we can get home without a tantrum."

Ella went to the back seat, but she felt unsettled. Should they really be playing Lacy's game, or should they be telling her that her mother and Arlo weren't really there? The fear of damaging her emotionally for life was very real. The little girl had been through a lot and the last thing Ella wanted to do was exacerbate the problem or increase the impact of her loss.

As soon as Tait unloaded the shopping and Lacy had her shoes off, Ella found herself easily coerced into climbing in and out of boxes which had become houses again. Anything was better than shopping with Lacy and her imaginary family.

This time 'Arlo' was playing with them and Ella was reprimanded a few times for leaving him outside. How long would it take to get the hang of playing with such an imagination? If only she'd studied childcare at Uni. There was so much more involved than she'd expected.

"Come," Lacy called as Ella struggled once more to follow her through a box too small for an adult.

A knock came at the door.

Her cheeks flamed red and she quickly scrambled backwards, very aware that her bottom poking from the box was visible from the door. She spun around to see Gabe. Heat warmed her cheeks.

"Having fun?" His tone was dry.

Ella frowned to hide her embarrassment. "You're back."

"I am." He pointed to the lock on the door. "Want to let me in?"

Lacy had heard his voice and was excitedly bouncing at the door. "Daddy, Daddy! Arlo and Mommy and me shop."

Gabe shot Ella a look.

"She's not talking about me." She came to the door and unlocked it. "She pretended Verity went with us to the shops today. And Arlo is her imaginary friend." A thought struck her. "That's unless she has a brother you and Verity forgot to tell me about?"

Gabe's jaw jumped and she bit her lip. That hadn't been necessary. Or kind. She didn't like the way she treated Gabe sometimes, but why was he avoiding her eyes instead of answering her question?

She opened the door and Lacy flew into her father's arms. He lifted her and held her tight, almost as though he was afraid to let her go. She clung right back and Ella let out a shaky sigh.

"So is there a brother? And is there a reason you're here almost as soon as you left?"

Gabe cringed. "I'm not going to talk about it in front of—" He tilted his head to the little girl still clinging to him.

Shame filled her. He was right. She shouldn't talk about Lacy and her imagination in front of her either. She had so much to learn about motherhood.

"We do need to talk, though."

His tone set Ella's heart pounding. Something was wrong. She could hear it in his voice and see it in his eyes.

Still holding Lacy, he took out his phone. "Mum, I've arrived. I'll drop Lacy up to you now, then I'll talk to Ella."

As Gabe left with Lacy and her new soft toy in his arms Ella felt as though another part of her was being torn away. What did Gabe have to say that was so important? He wouldn't take Lacy away from her, would he? Because she couldn't handle any more pain.

Chapter Twenty-Two

When Gabe returned he sat at the kitchen table, rubbing his finger along the edge. Finally, he looked at Ella. "About the brother thing ..."

She waited, keeping her expression neutral but dreading what he was about to say.

"Lacy has been pretending she has a brother for months. One of her friends in the States has a little brother and I think she got it into her head that she wanted one too."

Oh. Was that all? A relieved, hysterical giggle welled up. "What about monsters? You know any monsters?"

She'd thought Gabe would laugh, but he straightened, suddenly tense. "What do you mean?"

She related the story of the check-out girl.

Gabe's eyes darkened. "What did the girl look like?"

It seemed like a strange question, but she answered. She could see his mind ticking over. Why wouldn't he tell her what he was thinking? Surely the appearance of the check-out girl was insignificant?

Gabe leaned forward, his eyes capturing hers. She felt like a bookkeeper sitting before an auditor. His business suit was so perfectly fitted and ironed and his searching gaze was too intense.

"You can't do that again, Gabriella. You can't take her shopping."

She sat taller. "You can't order me around like that."

"They're not my orders."

"Yeah? Well Tait didn't have an issue—"

Her phone rang. She glanced at Gabe, then picked it up, still ruffled that he'd told her what to do.

"Ella, it's Detective Cooper. We have received intel that someone may be planning to abduct Lacy. There's no proof to the allegations yet, but—"

"What?" Was this what Gabe had been about to tell her?

Detective Cooper gave her a moment to take in the news. But she was in shock. How could he be so calm about it?

"And one of our suspects is missing."

"You have more than one?"

"Yes. Gabriel's business partner Orson Carnegie and his son Christopher."

She remembered her sketch. How Tait had asked her to age the suspect. It made sense if both father and son were suspects.

"Christopher has disappeared. Which means things are going to have to change for you and Lacy."

"Change how?" As if there hadn't already been enough change in recent days.

"For a start, there will be no more shopping excursions like you had this morning."

She glanced at Gabe, irritation welling up. He had obviously already spoken to the police about this.

"You will have security watching your cottage. They will walk with you wherever you go outside. You can go into town, but you can't take Lacy and you'll have someone with you."

"As in bodyguards?" Surely not. That sounded like overkill to her, but it didn't sound like she had much say in any of this.

"Yes. Gabriel has arranged some bodyguards. There will also be cameras and alarms installed. You'll have to inform the security team whenever you're going somewhere so they can go with you. And be very careful about keeping doors and windows locked. Am I clear?"

Shock gave way to anger. She gritted her teeth. "Very clear."

The detective ended the call and Ella thumped the phone back on the table and glared at Gabe. "So, you're doing the police's job for them now?" Sarcasm dripped from her voice. "They didn't do it well enough so you had to tell them what to do and use your own money to pay for added security guards?"

His jaw tightened. "This is their idea. And I agree with them."

"Well, I don't. You can't just come in here and tell me what to do. You want me to care for Lacy? To do what's best for her? Well, I don't want this kind of life for her. Or for me. Where's her childhood? Her freedom?"

Gabe frowned. "Ella, this is just the way it has to be for now. I'm not going to put Lacy's life at risk."

"Then quit your job. They probably just want to kidnap Lacy for a ransom or to keep you quiet about their shady business dealings. If you didn't have such a high position in the company and if you weren't so rich, this probably never would have happened in the first place. Give them no reason to think they can demand a ransom."

Gabe let out a scornful laugh. "Everything's so black and white, isn't it, Ella? Just quit my job and everything will go back to normal. Leave my employees high and dry, close the business, drop my money in a Salvation Army clothing bin, spend more time with my daughter and hey, why not just live it up while I'm at it?"

"No need to be sarcastic," she scowled. "You are living it up. You and your business suits and ties, your mansion in the US, your flashy car."

Something flickered across his face. So, she was right.

"And a private jet too?"

Gabe shook his head and the fire in his eyes died down to a weary blaze. "I truly don't believe they're after my money, El. They have their own. This is all about Monica and her deluded ideas about appearing young. There's nothing rational about it. But do you know how much I'd love to just drop it all right now? I'd love to rip off this choking tie and put on a pair of shorts and t-shirt—"

"Then do it. Just do it. You're not at work, now. You're here with me and Lacy."

He looked down, his expression turning sad and lost.

An urgent need grew to see him smile again, to make him laugh. She leaned across the table, putting on a fierce tone. "Take that tie off before I'm forced to take it off for you."

His eyebrows shot up, then one corner of his mouth lifted as he realised she was teasing.

"Really Ella? You think—"

She jumped up, raised an eyebrow and took a step toward him.

The corners of his eyes crinkled and finally, finally he smiled. "Alright, alright, it's going." His fingers worked on the knot of his tie. He threw it down on the table in front of her.

"The top button too. Undo it."

His brows shot up, but he did, then held his palms out. "Does that meet with your approval?'

Her heart lifted. "That's much better." If only he knew how much better. He looked a lot more like the casual, happy-go-lucky Gabe she used to know. The smile definitely helped.

"Seriously though, Ella," he said, "I need you to go along with me on this. Just until we know Lacy's safe."

"But what about the risk in the future? What about when someone else realises how rich you are and decides to try to take Lacy?"

"Ella," he said, and his voice was pleading. "One day at a time. I just need one day at a time right now. Can you give me that?"

She couldn't deny him when he looked at her that way. "I'll try."

His shoulders sagged with relief. "Thank you."

Now why couldn't she have just gone along with him in the first place? Why did she have to be so defensive and contrary? She didn't like that she put him through extra stress, but her emotions were all over the place and she couldn't seem to control them.

Margo arrived back at the cottage, Lacy in her arms. Her expression was apologetic as she handed Lacy back to Ella.

"I'm sorry you and Lacy have to go through this."

Ella glanced at Gabe who still sat across from her, fiddling with his discarded tie. Was Margo apologising for the new security measures and added stress that entailed, or for the way she knew her son had once again told her how to live her life?

Ella shrugged. "We'll get through it."

Gabe stood and straightened before holding his arms out to Lacy. "Let's go and meet the security team."

***

Ella reluctantly accepted the changes added security brought. Lacy was easy to entertain and thrived on attention. She smiled as Lacy came over, holding something out to her.

"What've you got, Lacy?"

It was the tie Gabe had left on the table yesterday.

"Thank you, sweetie. I'll give it back to Daddy when he comes." If he came. Sometimes he left with the police with no warning. She had no idea where he went or how long he'd be gone for. It made it hard to explain to Lacy. This whole secrecy business was driving her crazy.

Lacy pushed the tie into Ella's chest. "You." She tried to put it around Ella's neck.

"Me?" Ella laughed. "It's your daddy's. I don't wear ties."

Lacy sure knew how to do the puppy dog eyes, just like Gabe used to do. She even tilted her head and gave a few slow, hopeful blinks.

Ella tried to ignore it but gave up when she saw the slight quiver to the little girl's lower lip. With a shake of her head, she knelt down so Lacy could put the tie around her neck. Taking the two ends, Ella attempted to tie it in place. She had no idea how, but she had a fair go.

Lacy giggled in glee, bouncing up and down and waving her arms.

Ella had to laugh. It was delightfully easy to entertain a child.

A knock came at the door. Ella glanced down at the tie still around her neck. Flustered, her fingers fumbled with the knot.

"Ella? Lacy?" Gabe's voice came through the door. "I've come to say goodbye."

So he was leaving again. Lacy raced to the locked screen door.

"Won't be a moment." Ella darted a look around the room while desperately trying to wrench Gabe's tie from her neck. The action only served to tighten it further. Her fingers itched to cut the wretched thing, but she knew she couldn't. It was Gabe's. And who knew, it could have been a gift from Verity. Ella couldn't do that to him. She gave it one last pull. No good. And it was getting harder to breathe.

"Ella?" Gabe's voice came again. "You okay?"

Sheepishly, she came to the door to meet Gabe face to face.

"You right?" he began, then his gaze settled on the tie.

"I, um, it's stuck." She unlocked the door, embarrassed by how breathless she sounded.

Gabe stared, but his lips twitched. "You're wearing my tie?"

She managed a glare that dared him to ridicule her. "Lacy insisted I put it on."

"Okay. Well, that's different, then."

"No need to be sarcastic." And no need for her to be so defensive, but she felt ridiculous. Gabe managed to get inside despite Lacy clinging to his legs, and turned to face her.

"Can you breathe?"

"Not very well."

He came closer and his nimble fingers began working at the tie. He leaned down to work out the knot and she shivered as his breath warmed her cheek.

Then those eyes so close to hers smiled. "You think you did this thing up tight enough?"

She wanted to back away, but couldn't while his hands held the tie so firmly attached to her neck. It seemed to take a long time for him to loosen it and finally step back in triumph, the horrible thing held up for her to see.

"Done."

Breath escaped in a rush, but she felt anything but relief. More like a silly schoolgirl caught in her own trick. It had happened before, and most likely it would happen again.

"What do you do when I'm not around?" His eyes still held that amused look.

"What do you mean?"

"If I hadn't turned up, what would you have done about that tie?"

She lifted her chin in a stubborn gesture. "I would have managed quite well on my own. I have scissors."

"Well." He stepped back. "I'm sure you would have, but it might still be nice to say thank you."

Lacy looked up at him with a shy smile. "Thank you, Daddy."

He laughed and ruffled his daughter's hair. "I was talking to Ella, but I like your manners, Lacy."

Ella avoided his gaze. She didn't want to say thank you. Not like a little child who'd had to be reminded. But she needed to be a good example to Lacy.

He nodded once in the direction of Lacy then lifted one eyebrow at Ella. "What do you say?"

She glared.

He smirked back.

"Thank you," she gritted out.

The smile that filled his face made her chest feel tight. She wanted to hit him and hug him at the same time. It was good to see him smile again.

"You're very welcome." His gaze locked on hers.

"So you're leaving again?" She needed to break whatever was in the air between them.

"Yes. I'm sorry. I really don't want to, but Detective Cooper will pick me up in an hour. I'll be gone for a few days this time."

Probably back to the US. How nice for him that he could go home and not be stuck here all the time.

He followed her into the kitchen, hesitating as he looked at the pile of washing up waiting on her sink.

"I haven't had time to do it." She didn't know why she was so defensive.

"El, I'm not judging you. I was just realising how much I've asked of you. Looking after a two-year-old isn't easy." He shook his head and his tone lightened. "Especially when they require you to play games like hide-a-boo and cow rides."

"Cow rides?"

He went to the sink and began filling it. "Her latest. You haven't had to play it yet?"

"No."

"After we saw the cows, she decided I had to give her cow rides instead of horsey rides. It's completely changed the tone."

"From neigh to moo?" Ella tried to suppress the laugh that bubbled up.

He dropped the dirty cutlery into the sink. "Well, it's not quite a moo, but I'm not even going to try to make the sound for you."

Ella picked up a tea-towel.

His hands stilled in the sink. "You don't have to help. Sit down, have a rest." He looked at her. "Or you could always play cow rides with Lacy?"

She swatted him with the tea-towel. "You're the one going away. Go and play with her while I wash up. I promise I won't peek."

To her astonishment, his cheeks coloured. Was he embarrassed to play with his daughter in front of her? He clearly had no idea how endearing it was.

Only minutes later, squeals, laughter and mooing sounds came from the next room. Ella managed to keep her promise and not peek.

She had just finished the washing up when the two returned to the kitchen. Lacy was clinging to Gabe's leg and he reached down to lift her up. "You be good." He pushed a strand of hair from her face. "I'll be back as soon as I can."

She nodded happily, clearly not understanding. Ella wished she did. She wished Lacy would cling to him and beg him to stay. Instead Lacy giggled as he cuddled her. He then touched a finger to her nose before passing her back to Ella.

"Stay safe, El," he said softly, looking as though he couldn't decide whether or not to hug her goodbye. On impulse Ella stepped forward and put her arms around him so that a laughing Lacy was squished between them.

"You stay safe, too."

Chapter Twenty-Three

A knock came on Ella's door. She opened it, Lacy perched on her hip.

Tait stood there, surrounded by officers. Her heart sank as anxiety rose. She invited them in.

Nicola, the female officer, held out Ella's phone. "We need you to use your phone to ring Monica Langley-Moore. She's been trying to contact you."

Her stepmother? Ella took her phone, a symbol of the freedom and security she'd once had and lost.

"What do I say?"

Nicola indicated that Ella should sit down at the table. "Very little. We'll be recording everything. Whatever happens, we need her to think Verity is still alive."

"What about Lacy?" Ella perched on the edge of one of her dining chairs, her muscles tense as she pulled the little girl close.

"We've called Margo. She's on her way to collect her now."

Ella's hands felt clammy. What if she slipped up?

"You'll need to pretend you don't know who you're calling back," Tait said. "She hasn't left any messages and you clearly don't have her number in your phone."

"No. I haven't spoken to her since she left us when I was four."

Tait's expression turned sympathetic. He held out an earpiece. "I'll direct you as to what to say, how to answer her. I'll be in the next room."

Ella took it with shaking fingers.

Tait gave her a reassuring smile. "You'll do fine."

"Hellooo?" Margo's voice came through the door.

Reluctantly, Ella handed Lacy over to her, feeling as though another piece of security was being taken from her.

"I'll be praying for you," Margo whispered, and Ella felt warm again. If Margo prayed, surely God heard her?

She watched as the door closed behind them, then turned back to the officers.

"Nicola will stay with you," Tait said. "We'll be recording everything."

"What if I stuff up?"

Tait smiled. "We've got you, okay?"

Ella breathed out a long breath and wiped her hands down her jeans. "Okay, let's do this." Anything to find out what had happened to Verity and bring justice.

Nicola pressed in the number for her. The phone only rang once before someone picked up.

"Hello? Gabriella, is that you?"

"Yes. Who is this?"

Nicola gave her the thumbs up. The woman on the other end hesitated.

Then, "It's your mother."

Ella's mouth dropped open. She sat in stunned silence at the hypocrisy of the woman. Monica had refused to ever let her call her mother.

"Monica?" Tait's voice came over her earpiece.

"Monica?" Ella repeated over the phone.

"Yes, it's me. I'm really worried, Gabriella. I've been trying to contact Verity for weeks now and she hasn't returned my calls."

Anger burned inside like red hot coals being fanned by the wind. "Why would she, Monica? And why would I want to talk to you after all these years?"

There was another silence and Monica took a deep breath. "Verity and I have been in contact over the last ten years, Gabriella. She told me how you felt, that you didn't want to forgive me, but she feels differently."

Verity obviously did feel differently, and a renewed sense of betrayal swirled in Ella's chest. When they were younger, she and Verity had agreed never to speak to this woman again. If only ...

"Look, Gabriella, I know some things are hard for you to understand, but I do love you girls and I want to be part of your lives. Verity understood that and she let me be involved in Lacy's life, too."

At the cost of her life. But Ella couldn't let her know that. Her head was spinning as she tried to breathe.

"Have you heard from Verity?"

Her question brought Ella back to the present.

"Say no," Tait's voice said.

"No, Monica, I haven't heard from Verity for a long time."

Tait's voice came again. "Ask her if she's gone to Verity's home to check on her."

"Have you been to her house?" Ella asked. "To see if anyone's home?"

Again, that hesitation. Then, "She's not home."

"You went there?" Ella pressed, and Nicola gave her the thumbs up.

"Look don't worry about it," Monica said. "But if you hear from her, please let me know."

"Ask her how she got your number," Tait said.

Good question. Ella's hand squeezed around the phone. "How'd you get my number?"

"Verity gave it to me when I said I wanted to contact you."

"I thought you said you haven't seen her."

Nicola shook her head and Ella bit her lip. Oops.

"Oh Gabriella," Monica said, and her voice was sickeningly sweet. "What will it take for you to trust me? I want what's best for you and Verity and Lacy. I really do. It's sad that we've lost contact over the years."

Because you left us. She so badly wanted to say it, but she waited for Tait, eyes on Nicola.

"Tell me what I need to do to prove it, Gabriella. What do you need? Money? A mother figure? Do you want me to put in a good word for you with Verity and encourage her to get in contact with you again?"

Now Ella shook with rage. This woman had bribed Verity the same way, knowing her love of jewellery and offering to help her become an influencer.

Nicola touched her arm to get her attention. "End the call," she mouthed.

"Goodbye Monica." Ella hung up. She flung the phone onto the table and it rang again.

"Leave it," Tait's voice said through the earpiece.

Ella ripped the buds from her ears and dropped her head into her hands. The tightness in her chest expanded and heat burned her face.

"Go outside and yell," Nicola suggested.

"What if I never stop?" Her jaw shook with tension.

"You will. And I reckon you'll feel a lot better."

"Or you could pray," Tait said, coming into the room. "Let it all go. Lay it at Jesus' feet. If anyone knew injustice, if anyone knew loss, being misunderstood and mistreated, He did."

Ella ran her hands over her face. "I'm going for a walk. Alone."

No one tried to stop her, but she knew that if she looked back, a bodyguard or security guard, or whoever Gabe had hired, would be somewhere close by.

She power-walked, breathing hard, fuelled by anger and emotion. The further she walked, the more she began to hear the birds and feel the breeze again. She looked up at the hills. And felt warmth surround her. A presence she had felt before.

"God?" No answer. "I've got nothing left. I don't know what to do. I need you. Please."

In the silence she felt an answer. An assurance. He was there. Watching. Waiting.

Tait was waiting when she arrived back at the cottage. He handed her a hard-covered notebook.

"This was in Verity's luggage. We've copied it for our records and now we think you should read it. We didn't know your sister like you did, so you might be able to pick up on some clues we missed."

Her chest tightened. It felt so wrong to speak of Verity in the past tense. "What is it?" She turned the book over in her hands.

"Verity's journal."

Ella winced. "Tait ... I don't know if that's a good idea."

"Mommy?"

Ella looked up at the sound of Lacy's voice. She stood at her elbow looking at the journal. Was she calling Ella Mommy, or did she know the journal was Verity's? The little girl climbed into Ella's lap and stared at the journal. It occurred to Ella that it belonged to Gabe and Lacy now. And yet, she had known Verity for almost thirty years, even if she hadn't seen much of her for over a decade. Didn't that give her a right to it?

Tait watched her every move. "It might answer some of your questions and bring you some peace" he said, as though reading her thoughts. And he probably was.

"Thank you."

He stood. "I'll leave you to it."

Ella nodded. It was time for Lacy's nap but the toddler had decided she didn't need naps these last two days, despite being very grumpy and unreasonable by the end of the day. Today she'd fix the issue by lying in bed beside her, cuddling her until she fell asleep.

As Lacy's head nodded and her breathing evened, Ella cautiously lifted the cover of the journal and let it fall open. Her breath caught at the sight of Verity's familiar writing. It was as though a part of Verity remained here in these words, still living, still speaking. Slowly Ella moved her hand over the page, imagining Verity holding her pen, crafting each of those words in her flowing style. Verity was always so creative. The sweep of her pen stroke, her zest for life, even the way she swept her curls onto the top of her head had all spoken of her creativity.

She flipped through the pages to near the end of the journal where some words caught her attention.

I have been so blessed, Ella read, as Verity's voice spoke the words in her mind. She would say it with enthusiasm and feeling, her eyes shining with light and life.

Blessed? What did she think of blessings now?

I hardly know how to thank You, Lord.

Huh? Lord? As in God? She made it sound like she was a Christian like Tait.

But I will try. I wish I knew how to tell You how much I love you. But every word I have, You have given me. Every moment I live, You have given. I want every heartbeat, every breath to be for You. And even in my death, I want to live for You. I know my body will stop, but my soul can never die. And on the day I go to be with You, I will know what the real meaning of life truly is. I will leave behind this earthly body which so often lets me down, and go to be with You, the One who never leaves me or forsakes me.

Ella frowned. If this wasn't so clearly Verity's writing, she'd think she was reading someone else's journal. This was a side of Verity she hadn't known. So dependent on another, recognising weakness in herself and confessing it so openly. Desperation to see the Verity she had once known and loved made her want to weep. She needed some of her sister's confidence right now. But the only confidence she could see here was in Verity's God.

She flicked to the front of the journal, searching for the Verity she knew. A photo of a woman with heavy makeup stopped her. Something was familiar about her.

Lacy stirred, her eyelids lifting. Then she whimpered and turned to bury her head in Ella's shirt.

"Monster," she whispered in a frightened little voice.

"Shh, no, Lacy, you're just dreaming."

Lacy whimpered again, and Ella stared harder at the picture. She'd been trained to recognise facial features. This woman had blue, blue eyes. A sudden chill came over her as she studied the flawless skin and heavily made up face. Something was wrong. The face was too young for the expression behind the eyes. But the features were familiar.

"Monica?" she whispered.

"Monster," Lacy whimpered again, then raised frightened eyes to Ella's.

Ella's heart picked up its pace. The checkout girl had had bleached blonde hair and blue eyes, too. What had Monica done to Lacy?

"Why is she a monster?" she asked the little girl.

But Lacy buried her head further into Ella's chest. Ella knew she needed to wait. The moment Lacy fell back asleep, she put her into bed and called Tait.

Chapter Twenty-Four

Ella read late into the night. Tait was delighted with the new evidence Lacy's terror had given them, but it devastated Ella. Poor Lacy.

She found an entry Verity had written while she was expecting Lacy.

I'm so afraid, but I know You are with me, Lord. Like David when he went out to fight Goliath. He didn't look at himself and his weaknesses. He ignored the fact that he was a small boy only used to looking after sheep. He saw the power of God in him! He saw You, my father God. You won that battle for him, and You will win this battle for me. You are the mighty deliverer and You will deliver my child safely into this world. You will provide safety, all that my child needs. Protect my baby from those who would seek to own him or her for their own selfish gain, I pray.

The next entry was clearly written at a later date. The ink was black instead of blue and her writing was on a slightly different angle.

Nobody on this earth has loved me like Gabe loves me. I know he has his weaknesses, but he has many more strengths. He gives up so much for me and I love the way he loves little Lacy. His humour has me laughing so hard it hurts, his eyes have me lost in their depth and his whole being has me longing for his touch. I never dreamed life could be this wonderful.

Ella frowned. Verity did have a way with words, but did she mean what she wrote? Was it all part of an act? She read the next entry.

I tried calling Ella today. She didn't answer. Help me trust You with her, Lord. I long for her to know You as I know You. Please open her eyes. Be a father to her as You are to me. I would give up everything to have her know You. If it would take my death, I would give my life. You know that, Lord. But I don't need to do that, because You have already died for her. You love her even more than I do, and You gave Your life so that she could have a relationship with You, also. Show her that, I beg you. Show me how to reconnect with her.

Ella shook her head, the words slamming into her chest. Verity couldn't fake this, could she? The words so filled with genuine love?

And then another thought struck. Verity had said she'd be willing to give up her life it if meant Ella would turn to God. Had she known the arnica tea would kill her? Had she allowed it to happen, somehow thinking it would make Ella become a Christian? That would be so manipulative. So like Verity. Anger built red and hot in her chest. She refused to do anything else to please her sister. She'd done it all her life. She was done with that.

Except ... no. Verity hadn't known she'd die. Something deep within told her the truth. That Verity really had changed. She just didn't understand how or why. Maybe if she kept reading she would understand more. She pressed on, soaking up Verity's words.

You know my heart so completely, Lord – just like You knew David's. You knew the deepest thoughts of his soul; the sin that filled him with guilt and the thoughts so dark and shameful he couldn't bear to admit them. But when he confessed them he was set free. So Lord, set me free! Set me free from this awful competitive nature that caused me to seek to outdo Ella all my life. She so openly shared her heart and dreams with me and all I ever did was use it against her to take what she desired. I don't even know why I did it, but it always got me into trouble. It started so young. When she wanted to be a teacher, I decided I wanted the same. When she started writing, I decided I'd become a world-famous author. Then there were her dreams of boarding school; she so selflessly, graciously let me go without a complaint. I only asked to go so that I could outdo Ella. Then there were Ella's dreams of a husband and family. I only took Gabe because he really wanted Ella. And I knew Ella loved him too, she just didn't have the courage to let him know. She was too scared of rejection.

Ella dropped the journal. Good to know what her sister really thought of her. She wanted to stop reading, but the journal pulled her in.

I did have a crush on Gabe at first, but what happens when those childhood romantic notions fade? I feel so empty and it's hard work to love him these days. And what does he think of me now he knows the truth; that I'm not really like Ella at all and that I don't really even know what I am like? I've tried to be her for so long and now our lives have taken such different turns I'm on my own.

So forgive me, Lord. Show me who You want me to be. Teach me to love Gabe, to truly love Gabe. Don't let him suffer for my warped selfishness. And please don't let Ella suffer. Give her back what I took from her. Give her the significance she longs for, but don't let it be in achievements, in a husband, or family; let it be in You.

Forgive? How could God forgive such selfishness? Verity didn't even love Gabe. She didn't deserve him.

I'm so much like King David who took all that Uriah ever longed for and valued. I didn't care what I did to get what I wanted, or who I hurt. I just wanted it. Lord, cleanse me and I will be clean.

Ella skimmed further down and some words caught her attention.

Lacy. Unfaithful.

She backed up and read more carefully.

Gabe knows Lacy isn't his. I knew Christopher was using me, but God forgive me, I wanted to hurt Gabe. To hurt him for not loving me like he loved Ella. I can't believe how gracious Gabe has been, taking her on as his anyway.

Ella stared at what she had just read, sick to the stomach. Verity couldn't mean what she'd written could she? If it was true, how could she believe she was in heaven now?

"Oh, Vee," Ella moaned. "What have you done?"

No wonder Gabe had such a shadow around his eyes. No wonder he'd lost his boyish smile, the bounce in his step. It wasn't just that Verity had died. It was so much more than that.

"God," she whispered into the dark. "It hurts. It hurts so much."

She wanted to go outside, to look up at the stars, to feel God's presence, but she was afraid. Of what, she wasn't sure. She needed to have courage. To read from the beginning. Despite her dread of what she might find, she opened to the very first entry.

Jesus, You sacrificed everything for me on the cross and yet as You hung there dying, You still said, "Father forgive them." I don't deserve such forgiveness, but I need it. Oh, how I need You. I can't thank You enough for all You've done for me."

Jesus sacrificed everything for Verity? Ella frowned. She was the one who had sacrificed everything for Verity. And look how that had turned out.

She held the journal to her chest, as pain leaked from her eyes, down her cheeks and onto the blankets.

Chapter Twenty-Five

Ella woke to the too-bright sun streaming through her window. How could a day be so bright when the world felt so dark?

She forced herself to get up and feed Lacy breakfast, then fell onto the lounge, mind swirling with thoughts she couldn't process. A heavy sorrow had settled within and she didn't know how to shake it.

Lacy climbed up onto her lap and leaned against her chest. She lifted a hand to Ella's cheek. "Wet," she said.

Ella hadn't realised a tear had leaked out. "I know, sweetie, but I'll be okay." Or so she hoped.

Footfalls sounded on the gravel outside. Lacy slid off Ella's lap and toddled to the door to see who was coming.

"Daddy," Lacy's excited little voice called through the screen security door.

Ella wiped her eyes, then ran her hands down her jeans, trying to calm her heart. She went to the door and opened it. "Gabe. Welcome back." Clearly he hadn't been to the US if he was back so soon, but that also meant she hadn't had enough time to process what she now knew. Would he see it on her face?

"Thank you." His lips tweaked up for a millisecond and she studied him. It was as though she were looking at a stranger again.

What else had happened between Gabe and Verity in the last ten years? How many more secrets were there?

He followed her into the kitchen where they sat at the table.

Ella's heart was weighed down with the heaviness of all she'd read in the journal. But she needed to act normal. What would be natural to ask him? She drew in a deep breath. "Any developments?"

"Yes. I think the police are closing in on the truth."

The truth. Ella bit her lip to stop it trembling. Gabe looked more closely at her.

"El, is something wrong?"

The concern in his voice was her undoing. Her inability to love, to respond to him, had caused all this. Had driven him to Verity's arms. Had—no, she couldn't regret Lacy.

Gabe reached over and wrapped his warm fingers around her shaking hand. "Ella?"

"I'm sorry," she whispered. "I'm sorry I was so closed off, so self-protective. And I'm sorry Verity wasn't the sweet angel you thought she was."

Gabe's eyes widened, then his mouth tipped up in a wry smile and sadness filled the depth of his dark eyes. "I knew she was no angel, El. Just like she knew that about me. It's hard to have secrets when you're living together."

She shook her head. How could she tell him what she'd just found out? That Verity hadn't loved him, not like he deserved to be loved. That she'd been unfaithful.

Gabe looked at the journal on the table, then back to her. "Oh. You read it."

She nodded, and in that moment knew that he had, too. "You know Lacy's not yours?"

Gabe glanced toward the bedroom where Lacy's happy giggles sounded as she played with her toys. His mouth melted into a soft smile. "She's mine. Not my flesh and blood, but she's mine in every way that matters."

"When did you find out?"

"After Lacy was born. Verity confessed to me that Christopher Carnegie, Orson's son, had seduced her. Most likely at Monica's request. She was scared for Lacy, scared that Christopher would try to take her. She thought I would reject her, but I couldn't. She put my name on the birth certificate and we agreed that Lacy would always be mine."

"So why did you ask me to take care of her and even adopt her one day?"

Gabe's smile faltered. "She'll be safer that way. Monica's trying to take her. She knows I'm not Lacy's biological father and she wants to claim her. She says I'm not her real family."

Understanding dawned. "But I am. Biologically, I mean." He didn't want to give up Lacy, but out of love, he was willing to let her go and entrust her to Ella.

"I just wish I'd married Verity before this all happened," Gabe said. "It's one of my greatest regrets, that I didn't marry her before she died."

"So you did love her?"

He hesitated, then cleared his throat. "I learned how to love her." He looked down at the table. "I had been at breaking point, which led me back to church where I committed my life to God. Not because of what my parents believed, but because I knew deep in my soul that He's real and He loves me. He didn't take all my struggles away, but I knew He was with me, helping me through them. And as I grew to know Him better I learned what it means to choose to love someone." He looked up at her. "And I chose to love Verity." His eyes were telling her something, but she didn't know what.

She touched the cover of the journal. "What are you going to do with it?"

"Give it to Lacy when she's old enough."

With all of those ugly, awful truths in there? "No," Ella whispered. "You can't."

He bit his lip, gazing somewhere out the window. "Verity told me she planned to give it to Lacy someday."

Ella stared at him, aghast, and when his gaze came back to her, his lips curved in another almost-smile.

"I know, I know. I feel the same. I want Lacy to see her mother as sweet and angelic, a beautiful memory and example to follow. But Verity wanted Lacy to know the truth. She wanted to make sure Lacy won't make the same mistakes. And most of all she wanted Lacy to find the same forgiveness and peace that she did. She wanted her to know Jesus." His gaze intensified. "Just like she wanted you to. She was flying back here to see you, to tell you everything. She prayed every day that you would find the same peace we found."

And she'd died doing so. Ella shook her head, unable to take it in. She stood and began to pace. "How could God have let her sacrifice her life for me?"

Gabe rose from his chair and came to stand in front of her, bringing her to a standstill. "Is that what you think?"

"Oh Gabe, I don't know what to think." Tears welled in her eyes.

"El, that's not the way God works. He wouldn't kill your sister to get your attention. He's all goodness and love and forgiveness.

He already gave His life for you and that's enough. His sacrifice on the cross was once and for all."

She remembered the loving, comforting presence she'd felt as a child when she'd looked up at the stars. When she'd heard God's voice, felt Him. And she realised God had been getting her attention for a long time. A deep longing rose up within – a longing to know Him more. She wanted, no needed, God's peace. The peace Margo, Gabe and Verity had found. She was so tired of wrestling with her own thoughts, her doubts and fears. Emotion welled up.

"El?" Gabe touched her shoulder. "God loved Verity and He loves you, too." He shook his head. "I just wish I'd been living for God when we were teenagers, that I'd not wasted so much time."

Her throat burned. "And maybe if I'd listened to God I could have helped Vee, too." A devastating realisation hit. She, unknowingly, had contributed to the way Verity was. She had contributed to Gabe's pain. "Gabe, I've made so many mis-takes." She pressed her hands against her burning eyes. "When Verity was little I just wanted to make her happy. It made me feel worthwhile and like I deserved to be loved too. I thought I'd rejected Monica and her lies, but I was reinforcing them. I sacrificed myself for Verity, but she ended up the way she did because of the way I responded to her every whim and let her think the world revolved around her. All my self-sacrifice ... it had a devastating effect and now I can't fix that."

"But Jesus can." He spoke with such confidence.

"No, Gabe, it's too late." The weight of guilt pulled her down, all the lies she'd believed, the anger, resentment and denial. "Jesus sacrificed Himself and forgave her, but I sacrificed myself, then held it against her. I've been angry and resentful. And stubborn.

I ignored her all these years because of my bitterness. I made such a mess of everything."

He placed both hands on her shoulders, waiting until she looked at him. "I think you're being too hard on yourself. You should never have had to take on the role of mother to your little sister." He pushed a strand of hair back from her face. "It's not fair to expect a child to be a mother. That's on your dad and Monica, not on you."

A tiny flame of hope grew. She looked up at him, drawn into his dark eyes, the compelling truth held there.

"God can turn all things around for good, El. That's His specialty. I've seen it in my own life. If you put your trust in Him and believe He can turn death into life like He did at the cross, He will do it."

An image of the banner at Uni all those years ago filled her mind. *He is Risen.* Death to life.

"What do I need to do?"

"Believe," he said fervently.

"I do." She meant it with all her heart.

"Then do you want to tell God that? All you have to do is pray and tell Him you believe and want Him to give you a chance to start over, but with His help this time. Ask Him to forgive you for the mistakes, just like Verity did. There's nothing He won't forgive. And it will set you free."

"But how do I pray? What do I say?"

Gabe smiled. "There's no special words you have to say, you just speak from the heart. You talk to Him like you talk to me."

"Out loud?"

"Or in your heart. He hears." He must have seen her discomfort, her uncertainty, because he took her hand in his. "Would you like me to pray on your behalf?"

She nodded. Yes, oh yes, she wanted that so much.

He bowed his head, resting his forehead against hers, still holding her hand. "Lord Jesus, we believe. Ella and I believe. You know how much we mess up, but we know you love us. Please forgive us for all the mistakes we've made, all the wrong choices. We see the devastating effects and we are helpless to do anything about it. But we know You can bring life from death. You *have* brought life from death through Jesus. Please turn all our mistakes, our failures, around for good in the way only You can. And please help us now live for you, trusting you, learning to love you. Amen."

Ella blinked back tears. God had forgiven Verity and turned her sister's life around. She believed He would now do the same for her. Truly believed.

"Amen," she whispered.

A heavy weight lifted and hope for the future filled her soul. She closed her eyes, relishing the soothing balm displacing the chaos. Assurance. Stillness. Peace. Peace that far outweighed even that which she'd felt looking up at the stars as a child. Confidence that God loved her and would work this out somehow. And that one day she would see her sister again in heaven where there would be no more pain, no more baggage, no more competition.

She lifted her eyes heavenward and for a moment she could picture it so clearly it felt real. She and Verity were sitting on a rock in a beautiful garden, birds of brilliant colours singing in the branches of the trees. Verity picked a flower, the colours unlike any Ella had ever seen before, and handed it to her. A genuine gift of love with no hidden motive, no agenda. And there was Jesus, talking with them, his presence bringing light and joy. A taste of heaven. One day she was going to see her sister again.

Gabe gathered her into his arms, drawing her back to earth with a thump. She looked up at him, wide-eyed. Then he smiled at her, an understanding smile, full of joy, understanding and connection. And she found herself relaxing, allowing herself to lean against his solid chest.

"God's got this," Gabe whispered into her ear. "He's got us."

His arms around her were warm, safe, like God's love. His heart beat rhythmically beneath her ear, the steady, calming sound of life amidst chaos and death.

She exhaled, the last of her tension draining from her shoulders. "I know."

***

Gabe had left to see his mother several hours ago, but Ella's mind was still spinning, trying to process. She couldn't forget the feel of Gabe's arms around her. She'd seen God's love through his words and actions, but she'd also felt new sensations, feelings she'd never experienced before. What had she missed when she'd frozen at Gabe's touch all those years ago? Regret squeezed her heart. But no, she needed to trust God had this. That He had the world, the future in His loving hands.

God, please help me. And help Gabe too. He's still so weighed down by everything. I'd love to see him smile and have fun again like he used to back in High School. I'm so grateful for our renewed friendship though. Please help me to be the friend he needs right now.

She paused as Lacy toddled toward her, a book in her hands.

"Colour?" she asked, plopping a colouring book on her lap.

Bluey. Ella smiled as she looked at the cartoon dog. "Okay, let's put it up on the table and we can both colour."

They sat side by side, colouring in the characters from the Australian children's TV show. Ella knew it was Lacy's favourite and that she and Margo watched it together, but she hadn't yet seen it.

She was so absorbed in colouring that she jumped when Gabe knocked on the door. She let him in. His smile was warm and light as he came to join them at the table. Then he looked at the picture Ella had been colouring.

"What are you doing?" His eyes widened in horror, but the sparkle of amusement in them gave him away.

"Colouring in," she said, uncertainly.

"Well, I can see that, but the way you are doing it ..." He shook his head. "Just what are you teaching my daughter?"

His daughter. Her heart warmed at the way he claimed the little girl as his own despite everything.

"What do you mean?" She couldn't help her smile.

"This." He took the yellow pencil from Ella's hand and jabbed at Bluey's father's legs.

"What's wrong with that? I coloured inside the lines."

"Yes, but with the wrong colour. Everyone knows Bandit's legs are blue. It's Winnie the Pooh who is yellow. Isn't that right, Lacy?"

Lacy paused in her own colouring and nodded seriously, but her eyes held the same twinkle as Gabe's. She knew he was joking.

Ella shrugged and shoved the book toward Gabe. "Fine. You do it then."

She scraped back her chair and stood, but Gabe grabbed her hand and tugged it, drawing her back into the seat. He placed the book back in front of her.

"No, I think you need to give Bandit his dignity back. After all, you're the one who stole it."

Ella laughed, then with a shrug she took the blue pencil Lacy was holding out to her and wildly scribbled across Bandit's yellow legs, both inside the lines and out. They transformed into a mucky green. Then with a triumphant grin, she looked at Gabe.

And he laughed, a beautiful, free sound she hadn't heard since high school. "I think you need to go back to kindergarten, Gabriella Glade."

If only. What she wouldn't give for a chance to start over, to know what she knew now. And yet, as Gabe had said, God could turn anything around for good. Hadn't she only just prayed that Gabe would smile again? Hearing him laugh like that was a miracle. As was this rediscovered ease between them.

God, You gave me what I asked for and more. Thank you.

Chapter Twenty-Six

Tait and Nicola came to visit a few days later.

"Where's Lacy?" Nicola asked as Ella invited them in.

"Gabe took her for a walk to see the cows behind the main house. She's obsessed with them. And she always sleeps better when she's spent time with Gabe."

A look passed between Tait and Nicola.

"We need you to accept guardianship of Lacy as soon as you can," Nicola said, sitting at the table. "If you're willing."

"I'm willing, but I admit I'm worried about how she'll cope without Gabe around."

"You could always marry him." Tait smirked at her.

"Not funny."

"No, I'm serious."

Nicola looked between them. "Ella, even though Gabe's name is on the birth certificate, Monica has now legally contested his fatherhood. It seems that at some stage she took Lacy for a DNA test and the results have come back. We suspect she did it without Verity's permission, as the parental signature doesn't match Verity's, but the results still stand. Monica's partner's son, Christopher Carnegie is Lacy's real father. Christopher wants nothing to do with her, but both grandparents do. Of course, if Orson or Monica are found guilty of murder, that changes everything, but at this stage we don't have enough proof to charge either one of them."

Ella felt sick. No wonder Lacy thought Monica was a monster. Imagine forcing a little girl to have a blood test for your own selfish agenda. "But you do have *some* proof, right?"

"We do, and we're closing in." Tait glanced at Nicola. "There are three sets of prints on the bottle Verity drank from. Verity's, Monica's and Christopher Carnegie's. Our investigators are searching their home, looking for any evidence they bought the tea."

"I thought Christopher's father was the one who gave it to her."

"So did we," Nicola said, "but the CCTV footage showed that the suspect's walk was that of young man, even though he looked like Orson. And we still have no real proof of motive."

Ella breathed out a heavy sigh. *Please God, let this be over soon. Please protect Lacy from Monica.*

She thought back to when Monica had lived in her home. All the hurt, the fear, the feelings of inadequacy, the pain of rejection, the stinging words. It had impacted her for years, made her feel less-than. But no more. That was on Monica. On her selfish greed. No little girl should be made to feel that way, and she sure wasn't going to let Lacy ever feel that way.

"Do you know where you and Lacy plan to live once this is all over?" Nicola asked.

Ella blew out a breath, glanced at Tait as she said, "I'm praying about it."

His eyes questioned her and she gave him a quick nod and smile, sending him the silent message that she now believed, that she was a child of God. His face lit up in understanding and she looked forward to sharing more with him when she had time. "I still don't know if I should stay here in Australia with her, or move to Trinity Lakes in the US, like Gabe suggested."

Would Lacy cope without Gabe around? Would she? And even if she decided to go to the US, how long would it take to arrange a visa?

"Well, first let's get this paperwork done and submitted so that you're legally Lacy's guardian. Gabe has already signed his section and the sooner it's finalised, the safer Lacy will be."

***

Ella walked up to the main house with Tait. She told him about the change that had happened in her heart, how free she now felt.

Tait's eyes glistened. "That's amazing, Ella." He shook his head. "God is so, so good."

"He is." She smiled. "Margo has been so encouraging. She's been showing me some Bible verses and explaining them to me. And when I talk to God, I just feel so much better. Gabe said it's because I now have a friend I trust who I can talk to anytime, anywhere."

Tait studied her intently. "Might this change things between you and Gabe?"

"What do you mean?"

"Might you connect in a new and deeper way?"

She rolled her eyes at the meaningful look he was giving her. "You think I have feelings for him or something?"

Tait laughed and nudged her shoulder with his. "I did mean spiritually, but come on, Ella, I'm not blind."

That was for sure. He read people like no one else she knew. She was almost afraid to ask what he was seeing, but curiosity got the better of her. "What are you saying?"

He kicked a stone along the road, then stopped to look at her. "In the past you put up walls whenever Gabe was around. And it's not because you don't like him or trust him. It's because you were scared of allowing yourself to feel for him. But now ..."

"Now what?"

"As you grow to know Jesus more, and learn to walk with Him, you will have the same goals as Gabe, the same perspective. That means there is the possibility of a deeper love and trust between the two of you. Something special and yes, romantic too."

Ella cleared her throat. "It seems kind of warped to feel anything for your brother-in-law."

"He's not your brother-in-law. They weren't even married."

"No. But they were engaged and he chose to be Lacy's father."

"In spirit and heart."

Ella fell quiet, then cleared the lump in her throat. "Tait, he chose Verity over me."

"Once. Have you considered that his feelings might have changed? Or that things might not have been quite the way they seemed?"

Her heart jumped. "Why would you say that?" What did he know?

Tait chuckled and shook his head. "I'm just saying keep your heart open to new possibilities. Trust God. Trust He has your life in His hands and that He wants the very best for you."

She blew out a breath. "That was easier when I was a child. I used to look up at the stars and feel like God was there, that He was looking down on me."

"Ah, but that's the thing. God isn't looking down on us. He lifts us up to His level. When Jesus died on the cross and was raised to life again, He was raising us up to new life with Him. We can see the world the way He does, from His perspective and have Him as our closest friend and confidante. The Bible even says that when we believe, when we follow God, we shine like stars in this universe. *We* are the stars. We can watch the way He turns the world, knowing He knows what He's doing. We can be a light, pointing other people to Jesus, shining His love."

"We are the stars?" Ella tried to make sense of what Tait was saying.

"Like stars, anyway. It's symbolic. And it's not like those fake wannabe stars who love all the glitz and glamour and want to shine a light on themselves."

Like Monica.

"It's more of a glow. Humble and genuine, pointing to Jesus. Verity has been like that for you through her journal. She's sharing what God has done for her. She was sorry for everything and she was forgiven. She wouldn't want you to feel as though you owe her something. She'd want you to live in the freedom and love she found in Jesus."

"It still feels kind of wrong, though." Ella bit her lip. "Almost like I'm doing to Verity what she did to me. Stepping in as soon as there's an opening, when she can't fight for herself."

Tait shook his head. "You don't need to look after Verity anymore. She's safe in Jesus' arms. That means you're free to live your life. And if that includes loving Gabe..."

She shot him a look.

"You're scared," he said softly. "I get that. Love is a risky thing."

It was. Gabe had once had feelings for her. She understood that now. But that was a long time ago.

They arrived at the door of the main house and Tait turned to go. "I'll be praying for you," he said. And she knew he would be.

She knocked on the door, heart hammering in her chest, unsure if she was ready to face Gabe yet. Tait's words had shaken her, but also given her hope. To her relief, Margo answered.

Margo grinned as she let Ella in. "You'll never guess what our Lacy got up to."

"Uh oh. Tell me." Ella couldn't help smiling.

"She decided to colour in again instead of nap. She found the Zinc cream and painted herself and the walls."

"Oh no." Ella tried not to laugh. The Zinc cream had castor oil in it, used as a barrier for skin rashes. It was very hard to get off anything. "Where is she?"

Margo pointed to the bathroom. "Enter at your own risk."

"Knock, knock." She gently pushed open the bathroom door.

"Mommy El!" Lacy beamed at her.

Ella laughed. The little girl's hair was smeared in the cream, and her body wasn't much better. Gabe was squatting by the bath, trying to wash it off, but the oil and water mix was clearly thwarting his efforts.

He turned, eyes twinkling. "You find this funny?"

His playful tone set her at ease. "I admit I do. I mean, she's your daughter. It's time you had to deal with something like this."

"She gets it from you, though. I hear these things are most often inherited from Aunts."

"Oh, really? What things exactly?"

"Messiness, accidents, trouble."

"Is that so?" Ella gave him a gentle shove, knocking him off balance.

He fell forward, his shirt sleeves sinking into the bath, water splashing onto his face.

Her mouth fell open. Lacy giggled.

Gabe shook the water from his arms, ran his hands down his face then turned to face her. His shirt front was wet, too. "I think someone needs a big wet hug."

Ella eyed the doorway and backed away. "I'm sorry. I really am."

He searched her face, then nodded once before turning back to Lacy. And Ella felt bereft. She hadn't realised how badly she'd wanted to feel his arms around her again. Tait was right. She put up barriers. But she didn't need to anymore. Even if Gabe rejected her, God loved her. And Gabe certainly didn't appear to be rejecting her right now. He was just respecting her boundaries, the barriers she wanted to tear down.

"Well, I'm going," she said brightly, opening the door. "I mean, you just don't know what accidents might happen when you and Lacy are together. Like father like daughter, I say."

Gabe spun around and Ella took another step back.

Lacy giggled again as she patted his shirt front. "Wet, all wet," she said.

Gabe shook his head. "Two giggly, talkative females," he groaned. "And one of them flirting and attention-seeking by soaking me with bathwater in front of my impressionable daughter. How am I supposed to deal with this?"

Heat climbed up Ella's neck. "I wasn't flirting." Or was she?

"What does flirting mean to you, then?" He half-heartedly attempted to wring out his shirt sleeves.

"Whatever the dictionary says it means."

"Then you'd better look it up." One brow lifted in a challenge, then he smiled.

Her heart gave a crazy leap. Without answering, she pulled the door shut and escaped down the hall. Gabe Vance looking at her like that was unsettling.

Out in the hallway, she pulled out her phone and looked up 'flirt'.

To behave playfully toward someone you are attracted to.
Okay.

Gabe soon came out of the bathroom carrying Lacy who was snuggly wrapped in a towel, finally looking clean.

"You looked it up?" he asked.

She nodded sheepishly.

"You were flirting, weren't you?"

She cleared her throat and didn't answer.

His lips twitched as he moved past her to Lacy's room. Ella looked after them, hearing his deep voice talking to Lacy and Lacy chatting back and giggling.

They belonged together, Lacy and Gabe. She couldn't take Lacy away. But neither did she want to leave. The truth was, she was attracted to Gabe. Even after all these years. And that scared the life out of her.

Lacy ran back out of the room, now fully clothed, looking for Margo. Ella dared look into the room. Zinc still covered the walls and the bed had been stripped.

"You want help cleaning that up?"

Gabe tilted his head to the side. "Depends. Are you going to flirt with me again?"

"I didn't say I was flirting."

"Ah, but were you?"

She found herself caught up in his dark gaze, unable to look away. "Um. Well..." The words stuck in her throat.

A deep chuckle came from him before he came over and gave her an affectionate but slightly damp side-hug. "Right. Well, thanks for clearing that up."

She cleared her throat, then pulled back and pointed to the walls. "I think it might be more important to clear this up."

"I disagree," he said, but then pulled out some baby wipes and began to work on the walls.

"I'll go and get some warm water with detergent." She escaped the room. He was too close. Too attractive. Too, well, Gabe.

They finally finished cleaning and came into the lounge room to find Margo and Lacy still watching Bluey.

"Mommy El," Lacy said, jumping up to tug on Ella's hand, pulling her toward the lounge. "Cuddle?"

Ella smiled as she sat down and pulled Lacy into her lap. She drew her close to her chest, then looked at Gabe and Margo.

"I think we might need to come up with a suitable name for me if I'm going to be caring for her, something other than Mommy El."

Margo nodded. "I was thinking about that. "What about Mama? Sounds more Australian, and as she gets older she can change it to 'Mum.'"

Ella smiled and touched Lacy's cheek. "What about that? Can I be Mama?"

Lacy nodded. "Mama," she repeated.

"I like it." Ella wrapped her arms around Lacy, pulling her close.

Gabe nodded too, his eyes on Ella. "I like it a lot."

Chapter Twenty-Seven

"Ella, we found this on Verity's computer." Tait handed her a pile of paper bound into a book.

She took it and flipped through. "What is it?"

"It looks like your sister was beginning her autobiography. It's all in bits and pieces, but it's at least in chronological order. We've given a copy to Gabe as well."

"You want me to read it?"

"Yes. We want to know what rings true, what doesn't."

It was sad that they didn't know what to believe. But if Ella was honest, she didn't either. And she didn't know if she had the emotional strength to read more of her sister's words. What she might discover scared her.

God, please give me strength to read this.

"You don't have to," Tait said quietly. "We're going over it too. If it's too much …"

Ella straightened her shoulders. "No, I'll do it." Anything to help find the truth; to find the person who ended her sister's life.

Tait left, and Ella settled on the lounge. She read snippets of their childhood, and to her surprise, Verity openly detailed how she'd competed with Ella.

Maybe it was the feeling of abandonment that made me think I had to be extraordinary, Verity had written. *Knowing my mother had left me cut deep. She'd left Ella too, but she wasn't really Ella's mother. What kind of unlovable child must I have been for my own mother to leave me?*

"Oh Vee." Ella fought the burn in her throat. She'd never understood why Verity competed with her. Now she understood. At least to some extent.

Ella was my closest friend in the world. She never got upset with me. Never yelled at me, always put me first. And yet it never felt enough. There was still always this empty feeling inside. And so I tried to do better, be better. It was like an addiction. The more I achieved, the more I needed to excel. And to do that, to make myself feel better, I had to put Ella down. I knew she knew what I was doing, but she never called me out on it. And that made me feel worse.

Poor Verity. Ella skipped to where her sister had met Gabe, her heart pounding as she read the account.

I knew Ella loved him, so I wanted him. I saw the hurt in his eyes as he told me how he'd kissed Ella but she'd rejected him.

"She totally froze up," Gabe said. "Looked at me like I was repulsive."

"Oh, she's always been like that," I told him, seeing my chance to step in. "She's not very affectionate and she's always liked to be in control. She's got to be the boss of everything. Can you imagine what I've had to put up with growing up with her? Why do you think I went to boarding school? I needed a chance to be me without being controlled by my bossy older sister. She treats me like a child."

Ella swallowed hard as anger and betrayal fought against her love for her sister. "Lord Jesus, help me. Help me forgive."

She read on.

I am filled with shame and regret even as I write this. I knew every word I spoke was untrue, but more than anything, I needed to know I was better than Ella. More lovable. It's not that I didn't have feelings for Gabe – he was good looking and had the best smile – but my desire to have him love me was greater than my love for him.

I'd been with plenty of guys before in my need to feel loved, but Gabe was the first one who had principles and looked at me like a person with hopes and dreams, not just a pretty face. He said he wanted to know the real me. So I gave him the real me I thought he wanted. But even although his kisses left me breathless, he wouldn't go any further. I both admired and resented his physical self-control. He became a challenge to me. I knew that if I could get him to sleep with me, to go against his own morals, I could use that to hold onto him.

I knew I had to bide my time. All it took was a bit of alcohol and his parents being out for the night. We joked together about Ella's fear of alcohol, her fear of breaking the rules, and then we drank and kissed and became completely absorbed in each other and the pleasure of each other's touch.

Oh, Gabe. Ella's heart hurt. Alcohol had always been his weakness. And yet Ella hadn't seen him drink since returning to Australia. She didn't want to read on, but she needed to know the truth.

Once Gabe realised what we'd done, I saw the absolute devastation on his face.

"What's that look for?" I demanded. "Now you've got what you wanted you're going to dump me?"

"No," he tried to reassure me, "It's just I always planned to save myself for my wife."

I pulled him close. "Then let me be your wife."

"You're not even eighteen, Ella."

He realised his mistake the moment it left his mouth. How could he have called me Ella? I burst into tears and this time the pain in my heart was genuine. He begged and pleaded and apologised but refused to commit to marrying me.

The rejection angered me, so I put that anger to good use. I clung to him more tightly. Tried to keep him away from Ella.

But I knew he still loved her, missed her. And so I took it a step further. And I destroyed his life in an effort to hold onto him, to control him.

His parents were out and he'd invited me over for dinner. "I'm pregnant," I lied as he chopped up veggies for our dinner. His hand on the knife stilled and he turned to face me. I honestly thought he was going to fall over, the way the blood drained from his face. I didn't know someone with olive skin could go so pale.

"I don't want to tell anyone," I said, coming up behind him and wrapping my arms around his middle. Still, he didn't move.

"Don't freeze on me," I begged him. "Ella did that my whole life. You should know how it feels. If you reject me and this baby, I don't know what I'll do."

I actually managed to work myself up to really believe I was pregnant and was scared he'd leave. The tears in my eyes were genuine.

He put the knife down, turned around and pulled me into his arms. "Of course I won't reject you, but what are we going to do?"

I cleared my throat. "I've thought about it and I have an idea. How about I come to Melbourne with you? I'll take up a course down there near you, then no one need know. Not at first. And who knows, I might lose the baby. It happens a lot in first pregnancies." I didn't know if it was true, but it made it sound like I knew what I was talking about.

"Would your dad let you leave school?" Gabe still looked pale and I pulled him toward the couch and tugged him down beside me.

"He will." I could say it with confidence because whenever Dad said no to me, I'd pull out the Mum card. Say I'd contact Mum, ask if I could live with her.

Now Ella understood why Dad had allowed Verity to go to Melbourne. It had troubled and confused her at the time, but now it made complete sense. She read on.

Gabe's face filled with wonder as he touched my stomach. "Our child is in there?"

I smiled and pulled his head down to kiss him, avoiding another lie. I forced myself to imagine a baby within me, to make it real in my own mind so I wouldn't slip up. He promised he wouldn't tell Dad. I said I wasn't ready.

Of course Dad said I could go to Melbourne, but he also seemed troubled about it.

"Ella thinks I shouldn't let you go," he said one evening. "She thinks you're throwing away all your dreams. Are you sure about this?"

"Oh Dad." I threw my arms around his neck and kissed his cheek. "I've always known my own mind. And I'm not giving up my career dreams. I'm just chasing them with the man I love. What could be better than that? Gabe fully supports me. He knows I'm meant to be something extraordinary and make a difference in this world. He said so himself."

He hadn't, but it worked. Dad smiled and patted my cheek.

"Then okay, you can go, Verity. Chase your dreams with Gabe by your side. I've always liked him and wanted the very best for my daughters."

I didn't like the way he included Ella in his statement. It was my conscience bothering me, but I was too desensitised to recognise it at that time.

"Mama."

Ella pulled herself from what she was reading. Lacy stood at the door, rubbing sleepy eyes, her wispy hair poking out in all directions.

"Come here, sweetie." Ella opened her arms and Lacy raced into them. The feel of Lacy in her arms grounded her, and yet at the same time her emotions alternated between anger, horror, devastation and grief. Verity had appeared so ignorant of her own manipulative ways, but her writing showed a mature understanding of what was going on at the time.

Poor Gabe. He thought he was having a child way back when he was only eighteen. How terrifying and wonderful for him. But how could Verity have played with his heart like that?

She pushed the pages aside. She needed a break. Needed to get out for a walk. It would do both her and Lacy good.

Ella helped Lacy put on her shoes, then stilled. What was that sound? A buzzing noise somewhere outside.

"Stay here, Lace." She raced out the front door, to the gate. The noise was getting louder. And something smelled strange. Like burning.

"Ella! Get out! Now!"

Chapter Twenty-Eight

Ella's head jerked up to see Tait running toward her.

Nicola was on her phone, shouting orders to someone on the other end. She stopped mid-sentence. "Tait! Get down!"

Tait fell flat on the ground. A shot rang out.

What was going on? Chaos was erupting around her. Lacy! She had to keep Lacy safe. But where was safe? She darted a look around. A car tore down the road toward them. Gabe and Margo.

She looked back at the cottage, only to see bright orange flames licking the roof. On legs powered by fear, she charged back in the front door.

"Lacy! Where are you?" Silence. "Lace! Quick, come to Mama."

The awful sound of hissing and crackling in the roof met her ears. She stopped, straining her ears for as much as a whimper. Nothing. She ran into Lacy's room. Now wasn't the time to play hide-a-boo.

Please God, please, please ...

"Lacy! Lace!" Her own ears rang with her screams. She could hear voices outside calling her, telling her to get out. As if she would leave Lacy in here.

The front door was flung open and Gabe charged in. "Ella, get out. I'll find her."

"No! Gabe, I'm not leaving her." She coughed, the awful smell of smoke reaching her, burning her throat and eyes.

Gabe grabbed her arm, spun her to face him. "Trust me. Please." His voice cracked, his dark eyes pleading with her. "I can't lose you, too."

He'd already lost his father, lost Verity. What would it do to him if he lost her and Lacy too? Against every instinct, Ella turned and ran out the door. She needed to trust Gabe and to trust God.

Save them God, please, please save them.

Back out in the sunlight, in cleaner, fresher air, she was grabbed by Nicola who dragged her further from the cottage, away from the smoke. Everything within Ella wanted to go back in, but Nicola's calm voice ordered her to stay put and wait for the fire brigade. Some of the security team had grabbed hoses and connected them to taps. The small streams of water they pointed toward the roof didn't look anywhere near enough.

Ella stared at the increasing flames, at the smoke billowing in a toxic cloud from the roof. And then she fixed her eyes on the door, willing Gabe and Lacy to appear.

God, please. You can do anything. I know you made the world, I know you have the world in your hands. You died to save the world. Please now save Gabe and Lacy. Please, please ...

Her heart pounded, threatening to beat right out of her chest. She didn't know if the tears dripping down her cheeks were a result of the smoke or her fear for Gabe and Lacy.

It felt like forever, but it was less than a minute before Gabe charged from the house, head down, carrying a precious bundle. Lacy. Lacy's eyes were wide and frightened as she clung to her father, something clutched in her hands. Then she saw Ella and wriggled out of Gabe's arms.

"Mama."

"I'm here."

Gabe lowered Lacy to the ground and Ella threw her arms around her. Never had it felt so good to hold her. Then she saw what Lacy had in her hands. A ragged pink teddy bear with dark eyes, and Verity's typed up autobiography.

"Your book, Mama." She held it out.

"Oh, Lacy." Ella couldn't find the words. Lacy had risked her life to bring her a book she could easily have asked for another copy of. She drew in a ragged breath and felt Gabe's hand rest gently on her hair.

"Hey Ella, it's okay. She's safe."

She looked up. Met Gabe's tender gaze as fire lit her soul. "Oh Gabe, I was so scared I might lose you. Both of you. I couldn't bear to have that happen. You're my whole world."

The truth of her impulsive words struck her. She loved him. She loved Gabe. Not as a friend, but so much more than that. Love for him overflowed within, making her want to shout it to the world.

"You would have been okay," Gabe said softly. "No matter what happens, you always have God. He is enough. He'll never leave you."

His words doused the fire inside like the water eliminating the remaining flames in the cottage roof. Yes, God would always be there, but how she wanted Gabe to be as well. But Gabe would leave to go back to the US.

The sound of sirens filled the air as emergency vehicles roared down the road.

"We need you to come and get checked out by the paramedics," Nicola said, heading their way.

Ella looked up to see Tait being ushered into the back of an ambulance. She'd forgotten all about him.

"What happened to Tait? Was he shot?"

"No." Nicola pointed to where Tait now sat in the back of the ambulance looking as alert and watchful as ever. "As you can see, he's fine."

Fine was not a word that fit this situation. Emergency workers, including police, now swarmed the property. Firefighters stood outside the cottage, watching its smouldering roof. It looked like the fire was out.

A paramedic headed their way from the second ambulance and nodded at Lacy. "Is this the little girl who was in the cottage?"

Gabe lifted her into his arms. "Yes, this is Lacy."

"Come this way and we'll check her over."

Ella watched as Gabe climbed into the second ambulance and sat Lacy in his lap. It all felt surreal. She swayed as the adrenaline wore off, energy draining from her like a bath emptying of water.

Someone came to her side and led her to the ambulance Tait sat in. She fell into the seat while the paramedic took her blood pressure.

"You okay?" Tait asked, looking concerned.

"I should be asking you that question."

His chin dipped. "I'm fine."

Just as Nicola had said. Everything felt hazy, as though she were in a dream. "What happened, Tait? What's going on?"

"We're not sure yet."

She nodded toward the police combing the property. "What are they looking for?"

"The drone that dropped the firebomb."

"What? Was that buzzing sound a drone?"

"I was heading to your house when I noticed it." Tait heaved out a breath. "I turned and ran back away from the house when I realised, but it was too late. Nicola shot it down." He let out a dry laugh. "Impressive shot, too. By that time it was way over there." He pointed to where a group of officers now stood in a circle, looking at something on the ground.

"What do you think's going on?"

"I don't know, but I don't think you can stay here anymore. They'll probably put you in a motel overnight."

"What about Gabe and Margo?"

Tait smirked at her. "You ask that like you care."

"I do care." She slapped his arm, his tease breaking her from her daze. "Every life matters. I want them safe."

His grin softened. "They'll probably go to another motel, just until we find a safer place for you all."

Disappointment sat heavy in her chest. She wanted to be with them. She wanted to be with Gabe. Now that she'd realised she loved him, she never wanted to be away from him ever again.

Please Lord, you know my heart. Please make a way.

Chapter Twenty-Nine

Ella looked over at Lacy's sleeping form. She lay completely still, her tiny thumb resting in her mouth. The child was exhausted. Ella was too, but she couldn't sleep. Her newfound discovery of her feelings for Gabe was too unsettling. She glanced out the motel window to where Nicola stood on guard, then picked up the bound pages Lacy had risked her life to save. She opened it at random and began reading.

We'd been in Melbourne two months and my course was not what I'd dreamed it would be. There was too much theory and I was bored. I craved something more exciting, but I wanted Gabe as well. Ella and I had made a pact never to contact my mum, but I kept thinking about her; how she'd chased her dreams and not let anything stop her. So I called her. I hadn't heard from her in years, and she seemed very distant. I so desperately wanted her to love me, to treat me with more than indifference, and without thinking it through, I told her I was pregnant. Just like I hoped, but never thought would actually happen, she suddenly became all understanding and motherly. Her whole tone changed. She said she only went to the US because she wanted to make enough money for my future. Deep down I knew it wasn't true. I'd looked her up plenty of times and it was obvious she loved the spotlight even though she'd never actually made it as an actress and had only been in a couple of low budget Hollywood films. But she claimed she'd desperately wanted to keep in touch with me over the years but didn't want to interfere. She said she missed me every single day. I chose to believe her because I was so desperate for it to be true.

She begged me to come over and live near her so she could help me with the baby. She offered to set me up as an influencer alongside her and to pay for me to continue studying fashion and design so I could make my own jewellery one day. It felt like a dream come true.

But Gabe didn't want to go and I was too scared to go without him. I wasn't game to face my mother without Gabe by my side.

When I told my mother, she said her partner, Orson Carnegie, would give Gabe a job in his real-estate firm in Georgia and pay for his studies at the same time. He said if Gabe agreed to stay for five years after that, he'd make him a partner.

Still, Gabe didn't want to go, so I threatened to go without him and never let him see his baby. Finally he agreed, but he said that we needed to get married for the sake of our baby.

I promised that we would, as soon as I turned eighteen.

When we got to the US, Gabe signed the agreement with Orson Carnegie. Then I pretended I lost the baby. I thought Gabe would be relieved. I didn't expect the depth of his anguish. Nor my mother's reaction. I thought she'd comfort me, but she accused me of being careless and said it was all my fault. She was so angry at first that it scared me. She threatened to send me back to Australia without Gabe. But to my relief, a few days later she became all sweet again and said she still wanted to work with me, but that I needed to take on her name and pretend to be her sister. It was crazy, but I went along with it and began calling her Monica.

From then, Gabe sank into depression over the lost baby – who never existed. He spent hours studying and working and I could tell he was grieving. I missed him.

"Gabe, I need you," I pleaded with him. "I'm grieving too, but you're at work all the time. We can have another baby."

He just looked at me with those big, dark eyes full of sorrow. "I loved this one. You can't replace a child."

"But we didn't even know this child."

His eyes widened and he stared at me as though seeing me for the first time. As though he could see the darkness of my heart.

"Maybe we're being punished, Verity," he said. "Maybe this is God's punishment for sleeping with you outside of marriage. I knew better than that."

"But what's so wrong with that?" I pleaded with him. "Everyone does it."

He swallowed hard, then shook his head. "The God who made the stars, who calls each one by name, who created the heavens and the earth made us. He told us what is good, how best to live, and we've gone against that. We've made our own pit to fall into."

Ella stopped reading. The God who created the stars, called each one by name. It was a beautiful thought that took her back to her childhood. If only Verity had understood that too. She read on.

Fury filled me and I screamed at Gabe. "You're being ridiculous. I'm sick of your goody-two-shoes act, quoting the Bible or whatever it is at me. Stop hiding behind God. He doesn't care what we do."

"Ella, listen to me," he said, then realised his mistake. He'd called me Ella again. I threw a vase at him and went into my room and cried.

Ella winced. No wonder Verity was upset. But hope also filled her. Gabe had still thought of her. Even after he'd left. What was she supposed to make of that?

Then only a few days after I turned eighteen, I heard him talking on the phone to his mum. He said we got married. I couldn't believe it. Of all the hypocritical …

We had a huge fight. He said he needed to tell his mum we were married because she wouldn't understand us living together otherwise. I agreed to go along with it, but I used it against him every chance I got. If he didn't do what I wanted, I would threaten to tell his mum we weren't really married.

He hardly spoke to me from that day. We lived in the same house, but he slept in a different room and spent all his waking hours at work. Orson Carnegie, my mother's partner, was delighted with him. Said he was a quick learner with a brilliant business mind and that the customers loved and trusted him. He was raking in the money with Gabe there. He'd used his influence to get Gabe a visa and a real estate license. I'm not even sure if it was ethical.

Monica helped me set up my own hand-made jewellery business and I began making money of my own and spending a lot of time with her. She never felt like my mother; more of a friend, but the kind you didn't fully trust, who would always put herself and her own agenda first. The problem was, the more time I spent with her, the more I saw of myself. And I hated what I saw. It scared me.

I tried harder and harder to seduce Gabe again, but it was like he couldn't look at me. I knew that I couldn't blame it on the fact that he still loved Ella. I was an awful person and I knew it. I knew Gabe would have gone home to Australia if I hadn't convinced him to sign the agreement with Carnegie Real Estate when I pretended I was carrying his child.

I wanted to hurt Gabe as much as I felt hurt. I said awful things to him but he'd just look at me out of those big, dark, sad eyes and not react. It drove me crazy.

Ella bit her lip. She knew exactly what Gabe's sad eyes looked like now. The carefree teenager who'd become her best friend had grown into a man who'd experienced deep pain and loss.

Gabe was named partner and the real estate business became Carnegie & Vance Real Estate. At the celebration dinner, Gabe ignored me, but Orson Carnegie's son Christopher didn't. Christopher was good-looking but I knew he was a disappointment to his father. He was always broke and asking for more money. But that night, all I cared about was the attention he was showering on me. I wanted Gabe to see, to realise what he was missing by not loving me.

Many times I was tempted to go back home to Australia, but I couldn't face the shame. Everyone would know that I'd failed and that Gabe didn't love me. I was as stuck as he was. It was a complete mess.

And that night as I watched Gabe charm all his employees and associates, I allowed my mother to encourage me to have too much champagne.

"Come home with me," Christopher urged, and I felt I had no reason to decline. The alcohol helped numb the pain and altered my judgement. Christopher showed me the affection I'd been longing for. He was charming and persuasive and I couldn't resist him.

And then I found out I was pregnant. For real.

I thought about terminating the pregnancy, but then I remembered how devoted Gabe had been when I pretended to be pregnant, how much attention he'd paid me. Maybe if I convinced him it was his child, he'd finally agree to marry me. Finally love me.

I spiked his drink with vodka and convinced him we'd slept together. This time the child I was carrying was real, but still not his.

Ella sighed and closed her eyes. What an awful, horrible mess. She'd hoped that when Verity realised she didn't want to be like her mother she'd change. Instead she'd spiralled further.

When I announced to Gabe that I was pregnant and carrying his child, he finally proposed. He bought me an engagement ring, but he still seemed troubled. I hated that I had taken that happy-go-lucky nature he'd had when I first met him.

I tried to get him to move into my room, but he insisted on 'remaining pure' until we were actually married.

I couldn't help the mocking laugh that escaped me. "I think that ship has well and truly sailed, don't you?"

And that's when he told me he'd been going to church on Sundays and had found faith again. I'd thought he was merely working each Sunday as he always had in the past. But he said that after we'd slept together again he'd felt so guilty, he couldn't live with himself. He'd gone to church and talked to the pastor there. Then he'd confessed his sin to God, repented and been forgiven.

I accused Gabe of making God out to be some big ogre in the sky with old-fashioned values. He said that actually, he was discovering God was a God of grace and love.

I know it sounds crazy, but it devastated me. Once again, Gabe's love for someone else was stronger than his love for me. The feelings of abandonment left me battling depression. It was as though I'd fallen into a dark hole and every time I tried to pull myself up, I'd slip down the muddy sides again, landing in the muck at the bottom.

I was desperate to go and see Ella. She's the only one I ever felt really loved me. She put my needs first, sacrificed herself for me over and over again, even when I deliberately sabotaged her dreams.

But every time I talked to Monica about it, she'd remind me that Ella's mother died of deep vein thrombosis while travelling in a plane, and that pregnancy increases risk of clots. I resented the way she kept reminding me, but her words also made me afraid. What if I died? Death terrified me.

Ella shook her head. Monica's mind games were despicable. She wanted to throw the book across the room, but Verity's story reeled her back in.

As my pregnancy progressed, I talked more and more with Gabe. I saw that he really had changed. He'd made an effort to pull back on his work commitments, to spend time with me, to connect. And my guilt grew because this child growing within me wasn't truly his.

A week before the baby was born, I collapsed. My mother was with me and I have a vague recollection of her giving me what she said was Tylenol to help. I don't remember much from then except waking up in the hospital and trying to see through blurry eyes. I heard Gabe's voice first as I blinked, trying to clear my hazy vision.

"We thought we'd lost you," he said, and his voice was full of emotion. "I begged God to save you because you don't know Jesus yet. If you'd died ..."

He couldn't seem to go on. My head felt foggy and I tried to make sense of his words.

"What happened?" I asked the nurse, but my words came out all jumbled.

She smiled. "Congratulations, you have a beautiful baby girl."

"What?" Confusion swirled as I grasped at memories, trying to find the one where I'd given birth.

"You had pre-enclampsia – very high blood pressure," a woman I presumed to be the doctor said. "It caused a mild stroke so you may struggle to speak for a while, but we have complete confidence that

you will recover. Your left side has been affected, but we will make sure you have all the care you need. You don't need to worry about anything. Rest is the best thing for you right now."

Devastation filled Ella. Verity had a stroke? And no one had told her? She should have known, should have been there for her sister. Except a gentle voice deep inside reminded her it wasn't her job to change Verity. God had done that.

Suddenly desperate to come to the part where God changed Verity's heart, Ella skimmed the next few paragraphs.

At the time, I barely registered what the doctor was saying. I just knew something was terribly wrong. I remembered my mother advising me to have arnica to prevent clotting, but I'd looked it up and one website said it was unsafe as it could cause contractions. Now I wished I'd listened to my mother instead.

Gabe sat by my side almost constantly. His presence was comforting, and often I would hear him praying for me. Whenever he prayed, I felt peace. His deep voice had a soothing tone to it that made me feel safe.

I remember the first time the nurse brought me my little girl. Gabe told me later that they had to wait a whole week until I was strong enough to hold her. I don't remember the time span, but I do know I have never seen anything so beautiful in my life. She was sucking her thumb, making noises like a tiny kitten.

Gabe then held her and I saw the complete adoration on his face. He thought she was his.

We'd already discussed names and we knew she was Lacy. Our little girl Lacy Joy Vance.

My mother came in. "Why don't you take her back to the nursery?" she said to Gabe, and something in her voice scared me. It was too sweet. Too ... calculating. I wanted to beg Gabe to stay, but words were still hard to form.

My mother sat on my bed. "I'm so sorry this has happened," she said.

I didn't even try to talk, I just watched her every move.

"But don't worry," she said, smoothing back the hair from my forehead, "I'll make sure your daughter is cared for. I will take her as my own. Gabe won't want her once he realises she's not his, and Christopher isn't interested. I asked him."

I honestly thought I was dreaming. How did my mother know my baby wasn't Gabe's? She seemed to read my thoughts.

"Christopher told me. I paid him to leave you alone. To let you and Gabe be the parents, but now you've had a stroke, you don't need the stress of caring for a newborn baby. You won't have the strength and you need to focus on your recovery. If you leave Gabe's name off the birth certificate, it will be much easier for Orson and I to adopt her. It only makes sense, after all we're both the grandparents."

My head felt like it was going to burst. I remembered her once saying that having a child would help her image of youth. Surely she wasn't so evil that she'd set this all up? I closed my eyes, fighting against the bass drum thumping against my skull.

The machines beside me beeped and a nurse came in. She looked at my mother. "I'm sorry Monica, I'm going to need to ask you to leave. She needs to rest. Her blood pressure is dangerously high and we can't risk another stroke."

My mother laughed, a tinkling, irritating sound. "Oh, don't be silly. I'm the one who calms her. It was something her partner said that distressed her. Perhaps you can ask him to stay away?"

I tried to talk, but the words wouldn't come.

"It's okay," my mother said again, stroking my hair and I wished I could throw her hand off, but my arms felt like lead.

"I need you to leave," the nurse said firmly. "I need to call the doctor back in."

Mum did, but she was clearly reluctant. The nurse waited for my mother to leave, then called the doctor in. I couldn't hear what was being said while my head was screaming at me, but I tried to relax. I was too scared to die.

I called to God, and it was in that moment my eyes were opened to who my mother really is. She never loved me, never wanted me. She wanted my child so she could feel younger. That's why she was so angry when I pretended to lose the first fake pregnancy. That's why she was trying to get me away from Gabe. She was calculating, selfish and manipulative.

Like me.

And that's when I truly saw myself for who I really was. Calculating, selfish and manipulative. When Gabe came in, I was holding my newborn baby and sobbing my heart out. I felt as though my heart was breaking. I begged him for forgiveness. I confessed all my sins, told him that Lacy wasn't his.

The devastation I saw on his face was my undoing. But he didn't turn away. He told me about Jesus. He shared about God's sacrifice, His forgiveness. And as I gave the remnants of my putrid, broken life over to God, I felt myself being washed clean. I felt Him putting me back together, making me into the person He always intended me to be.

And there it was. The moment that had changed Verity. The news Verity had been travelling to Australia to tell her. Ella fell face down on the bed and wept for Verity's life, for her death, for all that was and could have been.

"Lord, tell Vee I forgive her. Please hug her close and tell her I can't wait to see her again."

Deep inside she knew it was true. One day she would see Verity again and all the baggage, all the pain, the misunderstandings, the failures, all their tears would be wiped away by Jesus.

Chapter Thirty

Ella awoke to a phone call.

"Hello Ella, it's Detective Cooper. There have been some developments and we need to talk to you ASAP. Can you be ready in half an hour? We'll be taking you to where you'll be staying with Gabe and Margo."

Ella's heart pounded. "I'll try." An hour would have been more comfortable. Lacy had experienced night terrors again. She remembered being interrupted from her reading by Lacy's screams, and then falling asleep.

She dragged herself out of bed, still in her clothes from the day before, then woke Lacy. To her relief, the toddler didn't seem too tired and bounced out of bed with a smile.

They were well and truly ready half an hour later when Detective Cooper knocked at the door. He gave them both a muffin, along with a cup of coffee for Ella and hustled them into his car. He took them down roads Ella had never seen before. They drove into a small town and were taken to a house hidden by tall trees that ran along the fence line. Security lined the driveway and some kind of device was being installed near the gates.

"What are they doing?" Ella asked.

"Installing a micro-doppler radar."

"A what?"

"Drone detection device."

Ella heart dropped as she remembered the smoke-blackened cottage, but her heart lifted again at the sight of Margo and Gabe waiting for them on the front patio of their new, temporary home.

Ella helped Lacy out of her booster seat and smiled as the little girl scrambled down and raced to Gabe. He swung her up into his arms for a hug. "Swing," she said, pointing to the swing set in the yard.

"I'll take her." Margo took Lacy and Ella was left looking at Gabe. This was the man who had been able to love Verity through all her deceit, to stand by her side and take her child as his own. He was stronger and more noble than she'd ever imagined. His integrity and honour were like a solid rock that could be depended upon, a foundation for the future that held up through life's storms, and yes, fires. She envied Verity the privilege she'd had of being chosen by him, of having his undivided loyalty.

To Ella's surprise, he drew her into a hug. "I'm so glad you're here."

She rested her head against his shoulder, warmth filling her. Could she dare to believe he might have feelings for her as Tait had suggested? Or was she deluding herself, allowing the longings of her own heart to cloud her judgment?

"You okay?" he asked.

She nodded. She was okay now.

Until Detective Cooper's voice reminded her why they were here. "Let's go inside."

She stepped into the house and stopped in surprise. Her belongings were piled up in the living room beside Lacy's.

"The firemen collected them from the cottage," Detective Cooper said. "Thankfully the fire remained in the roof and the water damage in the house was minimal."

Ella wished she could grab some clean clothes and go for a shower, but Detective Cooper was indicating they take a seat on the sofa. Her heart fluttered when Gabe sat close beside her, his shoulder resting against hers.

Detective Cooper sat across from them, looking serious as he leaned forward in his seat. "I've got some news."

Ella glanced at Gabe. Did he know what was coming? His expression said he was as curious as Ella was.

"Orson Carnegie turned himself in to police last night."

Gabe's eyebrows shot up. "For what?"

"He got scared. He found out his son had provided Verity with the arnica. He came clean about his business dealings because he's more willing to go down for that than accessory to murder."

"So Christopher killed Verity?"

"It appears that way, but we still can't find him. And Monica has arrived in Australia."

"What?" Ella's heart pounded hard against her chest. "Is she allowed to do that? Wouldn't you ... shouldn't she be arrested?"

"We don't yet have enough evidence against her to prove she was involved in Verity's murder. But that's where you come in."

"What do you mean?" Dread rose from her stomach, up into her chest and throat.

"We want you to call Monica. She's left a message on your phone asking to speak with you in person. We want you to arrange to meet her. We suspect she'll incriminate herself with whatever she has to say to you and then we can arrest her."

She drew in a fast breath. No. No, no.

"I know it won't be easy, but you can trust us, Ella. We will have people all around you, hidden but there. We'll keep you safe."

Could she do it? *Lord, should I?*

Peace filled her, along with the reminder that saying yes could see this whole ordeal finished. "I'll do it."

"No." Gabe's deep voice made her jump. "It's not worth it. This has gotten even more dangerous. What if—?"

"It's okay, Gabe." She touched his arm. "I need to do this. I want to be free."

And not just physically. She'd allowed Monica and her words to keep her prisoner her whole life. It was time to let God work in her heart, to live out the freedom God had given her, and prove Monica no longer had a hold over her.

She looked out the window at the hills. Her hope was in God. He would help her.

"There is one more thing," Detective Cooper said. "Tait will no longer be working with us."

Dismay filled her. "Why not?"

"His cover may have been blown. That drone with the firebomb had a camera and the attack was livestreamed to a site on the dark web."

"Why would they do that?"

"We suspect Christopher or Monica paid a hit man to take you out."

"Me?" Ella tried to fight the terror that filled her at the thought. Gabe took her hand and gently rubbed circles on the back of it with his thumb. If he meant it to calm her, it had the opposite effect. Butterflies set up a ridiculous fluttering in her stomach, and tingles flew up her arms.

"All of you," Detective Cooper said. "We believe the hit man was part of an organised crime syndicate. Criminals will do anything to find out who our undercover operatives are."

Gabe frowned. "So they were trying to kill two birds with one stone?"

"Exactly. But don't worry, we'll keep you safe. And we'll move Tait on and change his identity again."

"No." Ella's heart sank. "Is it really necessary to do that?" She hadn't realised how much she'd come to appreciate Tait. His steady companionship, his understanding and his faith.

"I'm afraid so. The image the drone captured of Tait is very clear. We can stop the threat on you more easily than we can stop the threat on Tait. We believe the threat on your lives comes from one source, whereas Tait's brother has so many criminal connections it will take years to stamp them all out. The Elliott family are well known and have a lot of power in the criminal world. And Tait's brother Joel will do anything to punish Tait for betraying him and testifying against him."

Ella tried not to worry. She could trust God with Tait's life as well as her own. After all, He was the God of miracles. He'd changed Tait from being a criminal by the name of Tanner Elliott, to a Christian who fought for justice. A dramatic change like Verity's. How could anyone not believe in God? The evidence of the way He worked in peoples' hearts was right in front of her. But what about in their circumstances? Did He change how the world turned, or did He just set it in motion and then sit back watching it?

"Will I be able to say goodbye to him?"

"We'll see what we can do." Detective Cooper met her gaze. "It will need to be quick. I'm sorry. It's for the safety of both of you."

"I know. But I still don't understand why Christopher would want to kill Verity. Or any of us."

Detective Cooper nodded. "It's something we're still not sure of either, but we believe we're closing in on the truth."

Truth. *Oh Lord, please bring the truth to light. Soon.*

***

Ella was relieved when Detective Cooper walked out the door. A magpie warbled outside and the soothing sounds of Margo and Lacy's voices out near the swing came in through the open door. She felt Gabe's gaze on her and managed to send him a smile. Which he didn't return. Instead, he gave her a searching look, concern written all over his face.

"Are you okay?"

"I think so." Well, she would be once this was all over.

"Your heart isn't too broken over Tait leaving?"

Did he think there was something more between her and Tait? She lifted her chin. "Only because I've lost a good friend."

Gabe's dark eyes bored into hers, then slowly, tentatively, he reached a hand to her hair. He touched the strands hanging over her shoulders. She hadn't even brushed it this morning. Her only hairbrush was somewhere in her pile of belongings on the floor. She pulled back, reaching to tidy the unruly tresses, but Gabe took her hand, gently holding it in his.

"Just for once, El, let it go." His eyes said more than his words.

She bit her lip. "What do you mean?"

"I mean, let it go. You don't have to hold it all together on your own anymore."

Was he saying what she thought he was saying? That if she fell apart, he would be there for her? How she longed for the freedom to express what she felt and be herself. To allow herself to feel, to cry out all the pain in the safety of someone else's arms. She craved it yet feared it.

"Oh, Gabe." She let her head fall forward onto his shoulder.

She felt his fingers gently combing through her hair, putting it in some semblance of order, and she wished for so much more with this man. For love, life and freedom. But she couldn't ask for that. Not yet. Not while everything was still so unsettled and their lives were still in danger. Now wasn't the time and place.

***

Later that afternoon Detective Cooper directed Ella through the phone call to Monica. They couldn't risk Monica hearing Lacy's voice so Ella had been taken to another location. Nicola was there for added support, but Ella missed Tait. And Gabe.

The mere sound of her step-mother's voice when she answered the phone on the first ring made Ella shiver.

"We need to meet," Monica said, her tone urgent. "I came to Australia to find Verity, and I've found out some things you need to know about your sister. I can't risk talking over the phone, so tell me where you are and I'll come to you."

Ella trembled with both anger and nerves, but forced herself to speak evenly under Detective Cooper's direction. "There's a church near where I am. I can meet you there."

Silence, then Monica sighed. "You still don't trust me, do you? I just want to help Verity and a private place would be safer."

"I feel safest in the church."

"Okay. Where is it?"

Ella named the church and town Detective Cooper gave her. He nodded his head in approval as she followed his prompts. He ensured Ella kept control of the conversation, not allowing herself to be swayed by Monica's manipulation.

"I can meet you there tomorrow afternoon," Ella said firmly. Monica argued for a while, then finally gave in.

"You did well," Detective Cooper assured her when the call ended. "Now let's wait for her to come to us. In the meantime, we'll search for her and Christopher and gather all the evidence we can. But I'm sure that when she's face to face with you she'll break and tell you everything. Then we can wrap this all up."

Ella sighed. The future was so unknown.

"We'll visit the church tomorrow morning to give you a feel of the place and plan out the details," Detective Cooper said.

Ella nodded, relieved when she was finally driven back to the new safe house. She was tired and emotionally spent and it was way past dinner time. She leaned back into the seat of the car and closed her eyes. Pictured Gabe, Lacy and Margo.

God, please protect us. Protect our family.

Her eyes shot open. *Her* family? What was she going to do? She wanted them to be a family, so very badly. All of them. She couldn't bear the thought of Gabe going his own separate way after this was over. Hated the thought that she wouldn't see him every day. She longed for him when he wasn't there. She'd been foolish to let him back into her heart this way. He'd shown that he cared, but he'd never said or done anything to suggest he would consider marrying her. Why would he after his experience with Verity?

She dragged herself from the car, her heart pounding at the sight of Gabe holding open the front door. The patio light illuminated his face, and her breath caught in her throat. Act normal. She needed to act normal or he would guess her feelings, her thoughts. He was no expert in body language like Tait, but he was sensitive to her feelings, her needs.

"Mum's bathing Lacy and putting her to bed upstairs," Gabe said quietly as she came inside. "You look wrecked."

She blew out a weary breath. "I am."

"Do you want some dinner? We saved you some."

For the first time she noticed the delicious scent wafting from the kitchen. "Yes please. It smells amazing."

"I cooked it myself." He shot her a half-smile as he led her to the dining table.

"Sure you did." She gave a weary chuckle as she sat down and pulled in her chair. Gabe found a plate in one of the cupboards then pulled a tray filled with beef, roast vegetables and gravy from the oven. It felt so right, being here, with Gabe.

He set the plate in front of her, then sat down across from her. He rested his hand on the table, palm side up. "I'll say grace."

She tentatively placed her hand in his open palm. He wrapped his fingers around hers and bowed his head. Every sense became aware of him, awakened and alive. Overwhelmed, she focused on the food in front of her. It looked delicious, but how was she going to eat with her stomach so full of butterflies that danced every time Gabe so much as looked her way?

"Amen," Gabe said and she realised she'd missed most of his prayer.

"Amen." *And Lord, help me. And yes, thank you for this food.*

Gabe squeezed her hand, then let it go. If only he'd stop looking at her like that, with eyes warm and filled with something almost tender. Something she didn't dare hope for.

She reached for the salt and knocked it over. Attempted to straighten it, but knocked over the pepper as well. Cheeks flaming, she tried to right it, and found her hand neatly captured by Gabe's again.

"El, what's wrong?"

She couldn't answer.

"Have I done something wrong?" His voice was filled with uncertainty. "You can tell me."

She made a half-hearted effort to pull her hand away, but he tightened his grasp and searched her face.

"It's ... it's not you," she managed. "I mean it is, but it's not your problem." Pain flashed through his eyes and she immediately regretted her tone. "I'm sorry. I don't mean it like that."

"You can tell me," he said, his voice deepening. "You know I care. I care so much it hurts. When you hurt, I hurt too. I want to be here for you and support you in any way I can."

What? Was he just saying that because what affected her affected Lacy too?

"I don't want to ruin everything," she whispered.

He stroked the back of her hand with his thumb. "I doubt that's possible. I promise to listen, to try to understand."

She swallowed hard. "Oh Gabe ..." What did she have to lose? "I can't see you as a brother no matter how hard I try." She licked suddenly dry lips, unable to look at him. "Somehow—I tried so hard not to—but I've fallen in love with you. Again. It's like I just can't help it. And then I panic, and so I put up walls again and I just can't seem to find ... who I really am. I've tried to fight these feelings, but I'm just so tired of fighting. I don't know if I can, anymore." Her voice broke and she slumped back in her chair. "I'm sorry. I understand if I can't be Lacy's guardian anymore."

He sat perfectly still, saying nothing while she stared at the pattern on the tablecloth.

She finally dared to look up and what she saw stopped her heart. Gabe was smiling, a full, complete smile. Not a boyish grin, but a deep, heartfelt expression of joy. Like the smile of his youth, but with warmth and tenderness that made it hard to breathe.

"Don't be sorry," he said, his voice low and husky. "I longed for this to happen. Prayed for it. But I never dreamed it was possible. El, I love you. I always have."

He loved her? Her heart pounded and she wanted to run. Anxiety threatened to overwhelm her, but she wasn't going to freeze this time.

God, help me please?

He stood, held out his hand in invitation. "Ella?"

She couldn't move. This was all too much to believe. She drew in a breath, trying to pull herself together, to hold back the storm of emotions threatening to break free and drench them both. "Gabe, I ... I can't think right now."

In a few short steps he stood before her. He placed his hands either side of her face and his eyes searched hers. Her breath caught as his head lowered and he brushed his lips lightly across hers. Every sense came alive, aware of him, aware of his touch.

"You okay?" he whispered.

She managed a nod. How could she explain the sweet sensations that coursed through her, the longing, the overwhelming joy that he would still love her, the relief that she didn't need to hold back her feelings any longer?

He smiled into her eyes, then kissed her again, this time more fervently, drawing her in, offering her his strength, his confidence and ... love. Making up for lost time. She found herself melting into his embrace, his kiss, driving out all fear and uncertainty. This was where she belonged. Here in Gabe's arms.

Chapter Thirty-One

Ella sat in the church, hands clasped tight as she looked around, taking in the layout of the building. Monica would be here this afternoon. Finally she'd face the woman who'd made her life miserable.

She looked up at the stained-glass window. Jesus smiled at her, a little lamb in His arms. It made her think of Lacy. Could she trust Jesus to protect Lacy?

"Ella?"

She spun around at the familiar, masculine voice. Joy filled her heart.

"Tait!" She ran down the aisle and threw her arms around him.

He stepped back, looking bemused. "Well, look who's gotten all gushy. And my name is really Tanner. You can call me that until I'm given my new identity."

She let out a shaky breath, unable to stop smiling. "Oh, it's so good to see you. I thought I might never see you again."

"Yeah, well you might not for a while, but Detective Cooper made a special allowance for me to be here today, to see this case wrapped up. And to say goodbye." He gave her a sad smile, then lifted his shoulders. "It's my job to read Monica's body language today. I'll see all her tells. We're almost there, Ella. I can feel it."

Relief filled her. Growing up in a family of criminals, Tanner had learned to read people to survive. Now he used that ability for good and Ella knew it was a gift. She'd never been more grateful for it than she was today. "Where will you be?"

"I can't tell you, because even if you don't mean to, you might look to the spot where I'm hiding. But don't worry, I'll be here and I won't take my eyes off you. Or her."

Detective Cooper approached, looking serious as he sat beside Ella. "Don't worry, Tanner's the best. Even if Monica doesn't confess anything to you, her body language will do the talking. It's almost over, Ella."

Tanner sat on her other side and she settled back into the chair feeling safe again. "So tell me how this is going to work."

Detective Cooper pulled out a piece of paper. "Most of our resources will be spent up at the house, protecting Margo and Lacy, ready to get them out at a moment's notice. Gabe will be there too."

"Okay." A band tightened around Ella's chest. Gabe had seemed distant this morning, as though their kiss last night had never happened. True, there was a lot going on to distract them, but it had left her feeling hurt and confused, unsure what to think. Had she been too cautious? Too needy? Or had it stirred up memories of Verity? Her chest's tightness reminded her of the day she'd realised Gabe had chosen her sister over her.

She blinked, forcing herself to focus on the task at hand. "What do I say to Monica?"

"Whatever you like. Just be you."

Ella tensed. She was still learning who that was, now she'd given her life to God and become a new person.

Once the plan had been laid out, Tanner touched her shoulder and pointed up to the cross. "He'll be here. Every step of the way."

She blinked. Jesus who'd died for her. Who'd died for her sister. For the world. He was the reason the world turned. She was going to trust Him in this.

She gazed at the cross, feeling her heart surrender. *Forgive me, Jesus, for all the times I didn't trust. For all the lies I believed. Help me have faith like Verity did.*

***

Later that day, Ella sat in the church, her head in her hands. She'd never felt this nervous in her life. Margo and Gabe had prayed with her and promised they'd be praying all afternoon.

She wished Gabe could be here by her side, supporting her. But he'd remained distant and hardly looked at her. Was he regretting their kiss? Or didn't he want Margo to know what had happened between them? Her heart twisted and she let out a heavy sigh. She needed to trust God with this. Even if Gabe rejected her, God hadn't.

Tanner was here somewhere, so well hidden she had no idea where. She looked up at the cross. She had to trust. There was no other choice. Margo had shown her a verse in the Bible before she'd left. It was from Psalm 121:1

I lift up my eyes to the hills-- where does my help come from? My help comes from the LORD, the Maker of heaven and earth.

He made the stars that twinkled at her in the sky. And she knew it was Him who'd wrapped her in warmth when she'd felt so alone, who'd whispered into her heart like a gentle breeze.

The sound of car tyres crunching on the gravel in the car park alerted Ella and she drew in a deep breath. This was it.

She waited, tense and ready.

"Gabriella?" Monica's familiar voice, now with the hint of an American accent, called through the church doors.

"In here." Ella stood.

Monica smiled as she walked down the aisle on high heels, but it was a tight smile that didn't reach her eyes. Make-up smothered her face, making her appear much younger than her years, and pearls adorned her neck. Ella wondered if they were real, or if they were as fake as Monica was.

"Gabriella." Monica nodded at her. "Thank you for seeing me."

Ella cautiously lowered herself into one of the front pews and Monica sat beside her. The woman's ice blue eyes met Ella's. Bile rose up in her throat.

Lord, help.

She straightened. She was not a vulnerable child any longer. Monica had no power over her. "What can I do for you?" she asked formally.

Monica tilted her head. "Well, haven't you grown some assertiveness?"

Ella stared her down.

"Right, well let's get to business then." Monica crossed her ankles. "I need to know where my daughter is."

"I told you, I haven't seen her for years. Or spoken to her."

"That's not what I asked you."

Heat rose up within. "Monica, you're the one who asked for this meeting. You said you had information about Verity. You don't want to push me, because I can walk right out of here any time I like."

Monica laughed, and the sound sent shivers down Ella's spine. It was the same laugh she'd dreaded as a child. The mocking, grating sound that left her feeling small and humiliated.

She looked up at the stained glass window, at Jesus holding the lamb. He'd protected her then. He'd protect her now.

Monica leaned forward, bringing her sneering face close to Ella's. Ella slid along the pew. "Space please."

Monica's eyes widened, the ice blue hardening to a glacial coldness. "Listen, Gabriella, I know all about you. Verity told me. We kept in contact even through your childhood. I knew all about your little whims, your little dreams and I helped Verity squash them. Better for everyone that you learned your place."

Ella didn't answer, tried to keep her face blank despite the sick feeling deep in her stomach. Her silence seemed to infuriate the woman further.

"If you have Lacy, I need her. She's in danger and I'm the best one to look after her."

"Why would I have Lacy and why would she be in danger?"

Monica came close. "Because you and I both know your sister took her own life. On a plane. In Australian airspace."

Ella gasped. "What? Why would you say that?" Hot tears of anger filled her eyes. This woman was cold. Heartless. Possibly even out of her mind. And she wanted to take Lacy.

"Do you seriously think I wouldn't be informed of my daughter's passing?" Monica shook her head and Ella was glad Tait was watching somewhere, reading through Monica's lies. Because she couldn't think, couldn't tell what was truth and what was fiction.

"I know you've got Lacy," Monica said. "You probably even tricked Verity into overdosing on arnica tea."

Oh, this woman was twisted. Ella clenched her fingers. "Why would I do such a thing?"

"Because you've always wanted whatever Verity has. You've always been jealous of her. But I'm the one with the closest ties to Lacy. You are nothing but a half-sister. Gabriel Vance is nothing but a spurned lover who can't produce children of his own."

Ella must have shown her shock because Monica smirked. "Yes, why do you think Verity refused to marry him? It's the only reason he wants Lacy. Didn't he tell you that?" Her eyes narrowed again. "But my husband and I are both the child's grandparents. Christopher Carnegie is Lacy's father. Orson Carnegie is her grandfather."

Ella closed her eyes. *Lord, help me!* Peace stole over her. "Really? Can you prove that?"

Monica swore, and her pupils dilated. Ella watched carefully. Was the woman mentally stable? She doubted it. Evil? Definitely.

"Yes, I can," Monica hissed, leaning forward and poking her finger in Ella's face. "A paternity test will solve everything."

"So why have you come to me?"

"Because it will be so much easier if you just hand the child over. Skip the messy court case. Do the right thing."

Movement came from the door of the church. Relief filled Ella. The police must have heard enough evidence. They must be moving in.

Monica turned to the door and a look of horror passed over her face. "Christopher. What are you doing here?"

The blood froze in Ella's veins as she slowly turned to look. Christopher Carnegie? Yes, she remembered those features she'd sketched. He stood at the door of the church looking wild and unkempt, his eyes fixed on Monica. But why weren't the police moving in? Arresting them both?

Christopher inched toward Monica like a leopard stalking its prey. "You told me I couldn't be charged with murder, Monica. You said that if Verity chose to drink the tea I couldn't be blamed because I never actually touched her."

"Christopher. Stop it. You're delusional." Monica's gaze darted around the room as though looking for an escape.

"Oh come on, Monica. Why don't you tell the truth? That you think paying me to seduce Verity means that Lacy is yours. You think you created her. That you own her. You're the one who's delusional."

Without warning, Christopher charged at Monica and his hands grasped the woman's throat. Her screams filled the air and in a flurry of movement, police appeared from every direction. Shaking, Ella watched as Christopher was pinned to the ground and Monica's hands were pulled behind her back.

The woman struggled and screeched but was quickly subdued and handcuffed. She turned to Ella, and the flames of hatred in her eyes burned through to Ella's heart.

"Gabriel Vance will never love you," she hissed. "He just wants Lacy. He always has. That's why Verity let him convince her to put his name on the birth certificate. When Gabe Vance kisses you, he's kissing Verity. Never forget that. You're her replacement. You always have been. Second best. Second choice."

Ella's chest tightened as she processed Monica's words. The woman was full of lies, but what if it was true?

"Ella, it's okay," Nicola said, coming to her side. "We've got them. You did good."

Ella rubbed clammy hands down her jeans and scanned the room. The adrenaline was wearing off and she felt shaky, edgy. She was desperate for space to think, desperate to escape. "Am I free now?" Her voice shook.

"You're safe."

"Can you drive me out of here? Now? I need to go somewhere. Anywhere."

Nicola looked at Detective Cooper who nodded. Then she put her arm around Ella and helped her to the car.

Chapter Thirty-Two

Ella sat on the back step of her dad's house, waiting for Nicola to arrive and update them on the case. It had been a week since Monica's arrest, a week since she'd last seen Gabe and Lacy and Margo. Ella missed them. Detective Cooper had explained there was to be no contact between them until everything was finalised and all charges officially laid. She couldn't help wondering where they were, what they were doing. Did Gabe think of her the way she so often thought of him? Did Lacy miss her or did she just assume she'd disappeared from her life the way Verity had? Had the papers declaring Ella as her legal guardian been processed, or had Gabe withdrawn them? So many unknowns.

She sighed and looked out at the hills. Dad had given her a set of watercolour paints, encouraged her to try something new. It would be nice to paint this view, to have a reminder that like King David in the Bible, her help came from God. She couldn't sketch God's face, but she could paint this breathtaking view; the one God had created at the beginning of time when he set the world in motion.

It was time for a fresh start. Yesterday they'd had a quiet memorial service for Verity. Just her and Dad. Barb, his partner, had gone to see her sister for a few days to give Ella and her dad time to reconnect, to grieve. She and Dad had cried together, connecting through their outpouring of grief. It had been sweet release and

Ella had hoped she'd find some sort of closure, but there were still too many unknowns.

A knock sounded on the front door, and Ella stood. Nicola was here. Perhaps whatever she had to say would bring the closure she needed.

In the living room, Nicola sat across from her and Dad, looking the most relaxed Ella had ever seen her. Hope lit a fire inside.

"It's over," Nicola said with a triumphant smile. "We have everything we need."

"It's really over?" Ella hardly dared believe it.

"It is." Nicola let out a huge breath. "I know it's been an incredibly difficult time for you, Ella, but you should be so proud of yourself. Your cooperation and your resilience have led to this case being wrapped up beautifully."

Dad looked at her, pride in his eyes and Ella swallowed hard. "Can you tell us everything?"

Nicola nodded. "I can. First, you should know it's been confirmed, that Verity was poisoned by arnica as we suspected. Orson and Christopher Carnegie were very happy to fill us in on everything when they were offered leniency on their sentences for doing so."

Ella held her breath. She wanted to know the truth and yet dreaded what she might hear.

Nicola leaned forward in her chair. "Monica wanted a child because she had some deluded idea that it would help her image. When Verity had the stroke but wouldn't agree to hand newborn Lacy over, Monica was furious."

Ella could imagine. Monica didn't like to be told 'No' and she didn't like anyone to get in the way of what she wanted.

"She even reported Verity and Gabe to Child Protective Services for supposedly being bad parents." Nicola screwed up her face in disgust. "Of course it was disregarded for lack of evidence. Verity refused to see her for some time, but recently, Monica convinced her she'd changed and Verity let her back into their lives. She even allowed Monica to take Lacy on a shopping trip without her. It seems that's when Monica arranged for Lacy to have blood taken for DNA testing."

Ella found herself trembling with suppressed rage. How she despised that woman. Poor Lacy.

"She then convinced Christopher to be a part of her evil scheme to take Verity out of the picture. She said that Verity was applying for child support from him and if he didn't end things now, it would never end. She told Christopher the tea would just make Verity peacefully go to sleep and never wake up. She said if he was caught giving her the bottle of tea, he could just say he didn't realise it was lethal."

"And Christopher believed her?"

Nicola nodded. "He has a learning disability and his drug use over the years has affected his mental capacity. Orson didn't realise how much Monica was taking advantage of that. But after Christopher gave Verity the tea, he panicked and confessed everything to his father. His father gave Christopher some money and used one of his private planes to help him disappear."

"And Christopher came to Australia."

"Yes."

"So he's the one who firebombed the cottage?"

"His dad had associates who found and paid a hit man. He panicked. It seems in his mind, getting rid of Lacy would get rid of any evidence, and it would also mean he would never have to pay child support for Lacy. So Monica's threat of him having to pay child support actually backfired."

Ella let out a breath and looked over at her father. His eyes were glistening with tears.

"Oh Dad." She leaned over and hugged him.

He shuddered out a breath. "I'm so sorry I married that woman," he said. "So sorry."

"It's okay, Dad." Ella desperately wanted to ease his guilt, his pain. "You couldn't have known. And without marrying her, you wouldn't have had Verity. You don't regret Vee, do you?"

Dad pinched the bridge of his nose. "No, but Ella, there's so much I haven't told you." He sighed. "I think it's time you knew the full story of what happened between Monica and I, but it can wait until later."

"No," Nicola said, "It might be best if you tell it now. It could help give us a better picture of who Monica is."

"You could be right." Dad looked from Nicola, back to Ella. "I first met Monica in the Morley Pub a year after I lost your mother. Monica had come to visit her grandmother in town and they'd had a huge fight because her grandmother wouldn't pay to support her and her dream of acting anymore. She had nowhere to go, so I invited her to stay with us. She seemed so moved by the fact that you had no mother and I was a widowed father. Anyway, she seemed so sweet. One thing led to another and she ended up pregnant. She wanted to abort, but I begged her not to. I convinced her to marry me by telling her that if she ever wanted to leave, that would mean half my money and assets would be hers. I never dreamed she'd actually leave though. I was a blind fool."

"So she took half of everything when she left?" Ella remembered back to that time. All the tension, the tears, Dad's grief, Verity's cries for her mother.

Dad nodded, looking defeated. "It took a while to get us back on our feet, but I managed to keep the house and keep you and Verity warm and fed."

Ella hadn't realised how much her father had been through. "Why didn't you tell us?"

"I guess I wanted to protect you." He rubbed at his knuckles. "And if I'm honest, I was protecting myself too. I was ashamed and humiliated. I know I wasn't a very good father, and I'm truly sorry for that."

"Oh Dad." Ella rested her head on his shoulder. "You're here now. That's what matters."

He patted her arm, then looked back at Nicola with a lopsided smile. "That's my story. Do you want to continue with your update?"

"No, I want to slap Monica's face."

Ella gasped and laughed at once. Was a police officer allowed to say something like that?

Nicola cleared her throat, a small smile peeking through. "Sorry, that wasn't very professional of me. Where was I up to?"

"Christopher's learning disability," Dad said. "But what I want to know, is why Verity accepted the bottle of tea from him."

"We wondered that too," Nicola admitted, "but her actions at the airport show that she never saw Christopher as a threat. Witnesses say that when he gave her the tea, Verity gave him a hug and thanked him. Gabe said she was quite open about her fear of flying and deep vein thrombosis so it wouldn't have seemed strange to her that Christopher might have wanted to help."

So Vee had simply been too trusting. Even she hadn't understood the depth of Monica's dark heart and evil schemes.

"Christopher says he almost changed his mind and even turned back around a couple of times as he was leaving the airport."

Ella almost felt sorry for Christopher. Almost. Then she remembered that he'd tried to kill Lacy. "Was it Christopher who sent me the package of arnica tea?"

"No, Monica arranged it with an old friend of hers as soon as she saw that a plane and passengers had been delayed in Australia due to death on board. She tried to call Verity and didn't get an answer, confirming that the arnica hadn't worked as quickly as she'd hoped. Verity dying in Australian airspace rather than the US messed up her plans to take Lacy. She won't tell us, but we think her plan was to make it look like Verity had made up the tea herself, and to hopefully take you out in the process."

The horrible woman. How could someone be so evil? "So what now?"

"First, there will be a trial. You won't need to attend, but Gabe will. As soon as Monica was arrested at the church, he was flown straight back to Georgia to help the police with their investigations into the murder. He also needs to wind down Carnegie & Vance Real Estate."

"It's closing?"

"Yes, but don't worry. Gabe's been found innocent of any wrongdoing, so his money is his own. He will also be able to reclaim the real estate business model he created as it was never used and he is part owner of the company. He's keen to find a job that doesn't take up so much of his time so he can be with Lacy. He's going to be fine."

Nicola's words slammed into Ella like a brick smashing through fragile glass. So that was it. Gabe didn't need to run his company anymore. He could look after Lacy himself. There was no need for Ella to be the little girl's guardian. Gabe and Lacy no longer needed her.

***

Ella shivered in the cold night air. She'd needed to get outside, to think. She'd tried to call Gabe now that she was allowed to, but he hadn't answered. She hoped he'd call back but dreaded it at the same time. What would he say? Would he be calling to say thank you and goodbye?

Monica's words had watered the seed of doubt that had already been planted. Did Gabe really love her? Or had he just needed her for Lacy? To make sure Lacy was truly his? Would he realise his feelings for her had all been driven by the intensity of the situation they'd found themselves in? They'd been stuck in a small bubble of protection, but now the the whole world was open to him again.

She wrapped her arms around her middle. "God? It hurts." Her sister had hurt Gabe so badly. Could he really forgive her, her family?

She looked up at the stars. She wanted to be like them. To shine for Jesus in the dark world. To see it all from His perspective. But facing Monica had shaken her, had taken her back to her childhood and all the questions, the feelings of inadequacy.

A car rounded the corner, its headlights shining on her as it drew near. Ella tensed as every sound magnified. She forced herself to relax. She was safe now, Nicola had said. And she had God. No matter what happened, she could trust Him.

The car pulled in the driveway. Someone got out and walked toward her. She squinted through the dark, trying to see. The walk was familiar. Strong, confident …

"El, it's me."

Her breath caught at the sound of the deep, familiar voice. Gabe! He'd come back. He was here. Her heart pounded and she stood frozen to the spot, watching him approach.

But as he came into the ray of light shining through the back window, confusion filled her. It wasn't Gabe.

Or was it? Memories stirred from a long time ago. This man was clean-shaven like the boy she'd known in high school. He wore jeans and a t-shirt. The suit was gone, as was the beard. He stopped in front of her and smiled tenderly, though a little uncertainly.

Her heart leapt as she gazed up at the face she knew and loved. Memories swirled, emotions ran wild. "It's really you."

"It's me." He smiled and her breath caught. She wanted to throw her arms around him, to cling to him and never let go, but she knew what she needed to say. She needed to let him back out gracefully. Trembling, she took a step back.

"Gabe, I've been thinking and praying about everything, and I want you to know I understand. I understand if you want to start fresh with Lacy, with me out of the picture. To move on from me and the connection with my family. I mean, if I hadn't been so … so cold and reserved, if the way I treated you hadn't pushed you into Verity's arms, which led you to Monica, and Orson Carnegie—"

He put out a hand to stop her. "El, it's okay. It really is." His dark eyes captured hers, begging her to believe him. "I can't regret any of it. All of that is what brought us to this point." He shook his head, a wry smile tipping his lips. "I was a child back then. Life was easy, I took it for granted, took you for granted. Now? Now I'm a man. Stronger because of the pain I've experienced. I know I need Jesus. I know He makes the world turn, that He's got me, He's got us in the palm of His hand. I know that He redeems what was lost, that He brings good from the worst evil we can imagine, that from pain He brings comfort and healing. He taught me to understand love. And He helped me understand you."

Moisture filled her eyes.

He reached for her hand. "I'm in love with you Ella. I always have been. You. Not anyone else. You. Just the way you are. You are the best thing that's ever happened to me. And Lacy."

She blinked away tears.

Gabe came closer, his eyes inviting, drawing her in. "I missed you," he said, his voice husky.

She'd missed him too. Oh, how she'd missed him. But if she spoke the words it would be her undoing.

"You can trust me, El."

"But ... but Verity ..." What was she trying to say? She didn't even know. It was just too good to be true. Too much to believe he might still love her. Still want her.

"Ella," he said, his tone filled with compassion, "when I kissed you, I was loving you, not Verity. No one else consumed my mind, my senses, just you. I've been careful, unsure if you were ready for me to love you." He gave a rueful smile. "Until Tait spoke to me. Tanner, I mean. He explained your body language, your reactions. He's observant, that man."

"What ... what did he see?"

"That you're scared. Scared of loving, scared of losing those you love."

"I *am* scared," she whispered. "And I feel inadequate. I've never been in a relationship before. Never been married..."

"I've never been married either. And yes, I've been in a relationship, but not with you. You're not Verity, so it's completely different. I'm in the same learning process you're in. But I do know this: I want you, Ella. Only you."

"But after we kissed ... well, you didn't talk to me, hardly looked at me ..." Tears filled her eyes.

"Oh El," his hand came up to tenderly touch her face, "I didn't want to scare you by going too fast. I thought you needed me to back off a bit. So much was happening, with Monica coming and the case coming to a close." He pushed the hair back from her face, wiped her tears with his thumbs. "I'm sorry," he whispered. "Sorry for all the misunderstandings, for my mistakes, for all your heartache ..."

She drew in a breath. His touch was so different from that of the boy Gabe. It had such a powerful effect on her. She didn't know what to do with it.

"Me, too, Gabe. I love you. I do want your touch, I just ..."

"I know." His hands slid to her waist and his dark eyes gazed into hers, questioning, imploring. He must have seen her answer there, because his head lowered until his lips covered hers in a tender kiss. There was no beard this time, just his lips against hers, softly moving, exploring, drawing her in, and she found herself melting into his embrace.

When he stepped back, Ella drew in a shaky breath, knowing her eyes were shining like his.

"Now I know that was my El kissing me," he said, his voice rough.

Hesitant at first, but desperate to be kissed that way again, she lifted her face. Delight shone in his eyes as he drew her close and kissed her as he never had before. And she knew without a doubt that up until now he had been holding back all the passion he felt.

When they pulled away to catch their breath, Gabe smiled into her eyes.

"I know someone else who's been missing you," he said. "Will you come home? To Lacy? To me?"

She blinked. "Where's home?"

He smiled wider. "I have another question to ask first." He took something from his pocket, then knelt on the ground before her. "Gabriella Glade, will you marry me?" Wonder filled her as the light glinted off the ring he held between his fingers. "Will you love me every day of this life on earth, the way it was always meant to be? Will you let your home, wherever you choose for that to be, become my home?"

Home. Oh, how she wanted a home with him. Tears of joy slipped out between her eyelids.

He rose from the ground to take both her hands in his. "Will you be Lacy's mother, and possibly mother to many more?

"I thought—"

"You thought what?"

"Monica said you can't have children."

"Another lie she made up."

"Oh." She should have known.

"I'm done with Carnegie & Vance Real Estate," he said. "I'm ready to start fresh. With you. Wherever you choose. Whichever country you choose." He smiled. "I'm kind of hoping you never let go of that dream cottage you drew back in high school."

She choked on a laugh. "No. I didn't."

He ran a finger down her cheek. "So will you share a cottage with me and Lacy, and have a cat and dog, a few chickens? And a cow for Lacy, of course. Can we live a peaceful, quiet life together?"

She chuckled. "Peaceful? I don't know about that, but I'll definitely marry you."

"And will you come to the Halley's Comet viewing party with me in 2061?"

She laughed, a free, full sound coming from a joy deep in her heart. "I'd love to."

Epilogue
SIX MONTHS LATER ...

Ella placed the framed wedding photo of her and Gabe on the sideboard Dad had made for them. A late wedding gift, he'd said. She ran her hand over the beautiful, sleek red gum surface.

"Is it how you dreamed it would be?" Gabe asked, coming up from behind and linking his arms around her middle.

"Better." She leaned back against his chest.

"I was talking about being married."

She smiled. "So was I." They'd been married a month, and Gabe was more than she'd ever dreamed. Steady, gentle, caring, faithful – a man she could trust with her life.

Gabe rested his chin on her hair. "The actual wedding day wasn't too bad, either."

Ella had to agree. It was a day she'd never forget. It had been a magnificent affair. Margo and Gabe had insisted.

"Neither of us have ever been married before," Gabe had reminded Ella. "I want everyone to share in our joy."

Gabe's friends from the US and all of Ella's work colleagues from the city had come, apart from Tait, who was unable to attend now he'd been given a new identity. She had, however, received a mysterious card and gift from someone by the name of Timothy Evans and she suspected it was Tait. It was a beautiful children's Bible for Lacy and a leather-covered family Bible for her and Gabe.

Ella prayed that one day he'd be released from witness protection and free to be himself, to be Tanner Elliott again.

She turned in Gabe's arms to face him.

"Now all we need is your dream home," he said, smiling into her eyes. "Somewhere we can live quietly, minding our own business."

She laughed. They were currently renting a house in the centre of Morley, a few doors down from Margo. It would have been perfect except for the couple living next door who often screamed at one another. There was never any guessing what they were fighting about; it was broadcast for the whole block to hear.

"You really don't want to go back to the US?" Ella asked Gabe.

"No. I like it here. Although I'd like to take you to visit some of my friends in Trinity Lakes one day." He hesitated. "And if you don't mind, I've been praying about it, and I don't want to have my own business. I want to keep working in Randall Real Estate here in Morley. I love being an employee, having more time to spend with you and Lacy ... and any other children God decides to give us."

Ella bit her lip, suppressing a smile. "So, no more rich, influential husband?"

He grinned. "We have a rich influential God. Isn't that enough? I just want to love you and Lacy, enjoy this life He's given me, and share His love. Money is over-rated."

"Says the rich man," Ella laughed.

"Hey." He drew her back into his arms. "Rich in love and God's blessings. That's what matters."

"It is," Ella agreed, sliding her hands around his waist. She heaved a deep, contented sigh. The Gabe Vance she knew and loved was here and she was in his arms, living life to the full.

A cry rent the air. Lacy.

Gabe reached Lacy's room first, Ella close behind. The little girl sat up in bed, damp hair plastered to her forehead and tears dripping down her cheeks.

"I had a nightmare," she said on a sob.

Immediately, Gabe knelt on the floor beside her while Ella sat on the edge of the bed. Now three years old, heading on to four, Lacy no longer had night terrors but her nightmares since moving into this rental house had been regular.

"Pray, Daddy?" she asked.

"Of course." Gabe drew the little girl to him and began to pray. His words asking for peace and comfort reminded Ella of a song they sang in church last Sunday. She still didn't like to sing in church. Singing triggered anxiety and had done so ever since her experience singing on stage on Verity's behalf as a fifteen-year-old.

But now, as she saw the fear in Lacy's eyes, a memory resurfaced. Her own mother singing to her when she was just a toddler. It had always brought comfort and a sense of being deeply loved. The need to sing for Lacy welled up within.

When Gabe finished praying, rather than leave the room, Ella took Lacy's hand. "Do you want me to sing you back to sleep? My mother used to do it when I was little."

Lacy's eyes lit up and she nodded, before leaning back against her pillow.

Ella couldn't look at Gabe or she would lose courage. It didn't matter what he thought of her singing, or if she messed up. This was for Lacy.

Her voice came out with a tremour, but steadied as she sang *Swept Away*, a song about God's eternal love, so strong no rushing waters or even death could overcome it. She came to the chorus and Gabe joined in, his voice deep and soft. Their voices blended perfectly as they both sang to Lacy about God's comforting presence, always with her, always loving, protecting and guiding her.

Lacy's eyes had closed somewhere between the last verse and chorus and she now breathed evenly.

Ella dared look across at Gabe. His eyes held wonder.

"I didn't know you could sing," he whispered. "You have a beautiful voice."

She opened her mouth to dismiss his compliment, but paused as God's still, small voice reminded her she didn't need to compare herself with Verity. With anyone.

"Thank you," she whispered back. She'd known from worship times in church that Gabe had a rich, deep baritone voice, but she'd never imagined they'd sound so good together. But God knew they would. He'd always planned for them to sing together to help calm their little girl; a little girl they had both adopted and claimed as their own, the way God had claimed them as His own beloved children.

Gabe stood and took her hand, leading her out to the lounge room.

"I don't think this house is the best place for us," Ella said as she sat down on the lounge. "I suspect the shouting next door triggers memories for her. I know what Monica was like ..."

Gabe nodded. "It's good that I found this, then." He pulled a blue binder folder out from the bookshelf then came and sat down beside her, his shoulder resting against hers. "It's given me some great ideas for building our dream home on the hill just out of town."

The folder looked familiar. "No." She gasped and laughed all at once. "You found my economics folder?"

He grinned. "I would say I re-discovered your dreams." He opened it and she laughed, reaching forward.

"Careful." He held her back. "Can't have you getting your fingers caught. I'll handle the clips." His lips twitched and his eyes sparkled with amusement as he opened the ring clips and pulled out two pieces of paper. One a sketch of her dream home, the other the newspaper cutout of him as a teenager with the beard and age lines Ella had added.

"Not a bad prediction," he said, holding it up beside his face. "What do you think?"

She laughed, reaching for it. "It's terrible. Look, the lines are all wrong, the shading is totally out —"

"Hey, hey," he pushed her hand away. "I get that you've had years of experience now, but it's pretty good for raw talent." He looked at the sketch of her dream house. "Seven bedrooms, El? How many children do you want?"

Ella chuckled, embarrassed by her memories. "Back then, at least ten. Now? Now I think it would be nice to take in anyone coming out of witness protection who might need a place to start again. Anyone who might need some love and care, some space to look out at the stars and consider who made them."

Gabe's eyes softened. "He's been good to us, hasn't He?"

"So good." Ella felt the tears stinging her eyes and let them fall. No need to hold them back anymore. She was free to be her. Free to be the person God was making her to be. Jesus had sacrificed His life so that she could have life to the full. Not pain free, not easy, but full because He was with her, always, working all things together for good. Not just turning the world, but alive and working in hearts everywhere, every day.

Gabe leaned over and pulled her into his arms, searching her face. "Am I allowed to kiss you?" he asked, his lips moving against her cheek. "Or might I get glared at?"

"Oh, Gabe Vance, grow a beard."

He laughed. "I just might. Again."

She laughed with him, joy and wonder filling her at the way God had blessed her beyond her wildest dreams. "I'd prefer you kissed me," she said.

"With pleasure." Then he kissed her, soft and slow, reminding her why she loved this man. God had given her so much more than her dreams. Her world had been turned upside down, but God had held onto her every step of the way, and He'd always be there. He was the one who made the world turn and she could trust Him. Completely.

A note from the author

I hope you enjoyed 'How the World Turns'.

If you'd like to read more about Tait Ellison (Tanner Elliott), he will have his own story in my third Trinity Lakes book due for release in 2025. You can pre-order "Like Stars that Shine" here:

https://books2read.com/likestarsthatshine/

Tanner also features in a previous story in my Bateman Family Novels. If you'd like to hear more of his story leading up to this one, you can read "Seeing Jess":

https://books2read.com/SeeingJess

Fun fact about the Facebook *Halley's Comet Viewing Party* that is planned for the year 2061: It truly does exist and has been set up on Facebook. I have marked myself as *Interested* in going. If you decide to go, I may just see you there :) Here is the link:

https://www.facebook.com/events/namadgi-national-park/halleys-comet-viewing-party/111707232941492/

I have referred to a few Bible verses throughout my story. I'm aware that it's always good to read these verses in context and so I have listed them below with their book, chapter and verse reference so you can read them for yourself:

Shining like stars – Philippians 2:14-16

Do everything without grumbling or arguing, so that you may become blameless and pure, "children of God without fault in a warped and crooked generation." Then you will shine among them like stars in the sky as you hold firmly to the word of life.

All things work together for good – Romans 8:28

And we know that in all things God works for the good of those who love him, who have been called according to his purpose.

Lift my eyes to the hills – Psalm 121:1-2

I lift up my eyes to the hills— where does my help come from? My help comes from the Lord, the Maker of heaven and earth.

Thank you for reading this story. May you know God's blessings, His help, presence and joy in your life.

Jenny xx

You can find out more about Jenny and her writing on her website: www.jennyglazebrook.com

Acknowledgements

I am so blessed to have an amazing team around me who critique, proofread, edit and beta read my stories. I thank God for every one of you.

In particular I'd like to thank Carolyn Miller for her priceless mentoring, editing, and encouragement. I have learned so much from you. Thank you for sharing your extensive experience, skills and gifting. I appreciate you more than I can say.

Thank you to my beta readers, Melanie Koch, Jenny Blake, Kaye Johnson, Lauren Gailey, Meredith Resce, Margaret Holahan and Rachel Dean. I love how God connects us with people at just the right time. Rachel was a friend from the small church I attended growing up. Even as a child she was always keen to read my stories (handwritten in notebooks) and encouraged me with her eagerness to read my work. I can't express how much it meant to have that support and I love that she is now reading my pre-published works again and offering so much valuable insight.

I'd also like to thank my family. My husband Rob, for reading the many drafts of all my manuscripts and encouraging and supporting me along the way. My children, for either reading this story and giving insightful suggestions, or allowing me to be lost in my world of writing for hours at a time. Also, thank you to my mother, Denise Crooks – for your proofreading and encouragement, my sister-in-law Helen Phillips for making some great suggestions and to my niece, Anna Irish for doing such a great job on the final proofread.

Most importantly, I thank my Lord and Saviour, Jesus, for giving me hope, purpose and life. I am so blessed to be able to use the writing gift He has given me as both worship of Him and encouragement for others. He makes my life rich and beautiful and His presence brings such joy and hope, deepening my faith through every trial.

About the author

J enny Glazebrook lives in a small country town in Australia. She and her husband Rob have four children and many pets who fill their lives with joy.

Jenny writes stories which capture what it means to know Jesus and live for Him in a broken world.

She has a Diploma of Theology, is a qualified chaplain and experienced inspirational speaker. She loves to encourage others to understand God's love, see His hand in their lives, and walk with Him each day.

More about Jenny can be found on her website at:
www.jennyglazebrook.com

Also by this author

AUSSIE SKY SERIES (YA fiction)

Blaze in the Storm
Heart of Thunder
Clouds of Prayer
Mist of the Morning
Clinging to Rainbows
Forgiving Sky

***

BATEMAN FAMILY NOVELS (YA/new adult fiction)

Daring Clare
Saving Beth
Framing Fleur
Seeing Jess
Living Melody
Loving Zoe

TRINITY LAKES SERIES (Christian romance)

Where Our Hearts Lie
In Truth and Love
Like Stars that Shine (coming April 2025)

***

OTHER BOOKS
How The World Turns
Molly the Dog-Sheep & other true pet parables (coming soon)

***

COLLABORATIVE WORKS

Wellspring Devotional Journal
Dear Jesus Diaries

**More about Jenny her books can be found at
www.jennyglazebrook.com**